"Patrick Hueller's *Me and Agent E* consists entirely of dialogue. But what dialogue--mostly between a father and his new baby, who happens to be a secret agent. The conceit is zany, even goofy, but at the same time, oddly perceptive and provocative. And the laughs keep coming in this innovative, engaging novel." -- Michael Fedo, author of *Don't Quit Your Day Job: The Adventures of a Midlist Author*

"Do you have a baby at home? Were you at some point in time a baby yourself? If so, you will want to read *Me & Agent E*, in which Patrick Hueller asks crucial parenting questions: why do newborns "punk" their parents? Are babies secretly in the employ of undercover agencies? What does it mean when a toddler's first word is "barnacle"? *Me & Agent E* is a laugh-out-loud experience -- and a tender-hearted good time." -- Julie Schumacher, Thurber Award-winning author of *Dear Committee Members* and *The Shakespeare Requirement*

"I really enjoyed reading 'Me and Agent E'. I thought it was very funny, uniquely written, and quite original with the family of characters and their relationships with each other. As a father myself, I know what it's like to have your newborn baby's life all planned out, even before they're born! This story delightfully brought me back to when my (now grown) children were infants, and I was a new father. While reading, I found that I was wishing for an 'Agent E' of my own, then realizing I have an 'Agent O', 'Agent N', and 'Agent A.' Well done, Patrick!" -- Rick Logan, winner of Acme Comedy's Funniest Person in the Twin Cities contest

Me & Agent E
By Patrick Hueller

For the real Agent E.

Paul

"What are you doing, Amy?"

"Calling my dad."

"Why?"

"Do you know how to fix a flat tire?"

"Why wouldn't I know how to fix a flat tire?"

"Why would you? I don't."

"It's just a flat tire."

"Oh. I see."

"What?"

"Because you're a man, you were born knowing how to fix a flat tire."

"That's not what I said."

"God. I didn't know you were such a chauvinist."

"Why would knowing how to change a tire make me a chauvinist?"

"*Do* you know how to do it?"

"Besides, *you're* the one who's calling your dad."

"What's that supposed to mean?"

"Why call your dad instead of your mom? Why assume he's better at it than she is?"

"Because, Paul, I know my mom and dad. I lived with them for 18 years, remember? My dad literally trains Eagle Scouts."

"This is a flat tire. This isn't starting a fire with a single match."

"What are you doing?"

"Calling your mom to see if she can help."

"What are you really doing?"

"YouTubing 'How to Change a Tire'."

Paul

"Now I can teach her how to fix a flat herself."

"Who?"

"Agent E."

"Stop that, Paul."

"What?"

"Touching my stomach. Didn't you know you're not supposed to randomly touch a pregnant woman's stomach?"

"That rule applies to husbands?"

"The Supreme Court is expected to render their verdict any day now."

"I will abide by the law of the land. Scout's honor."

"You're not a scout."

"I could be. Ask your dad if there's a badge for changing a tire. It'll definitely be part of Agent E's training."

"*Stop* that."

"What? I didn't touch your stomach."

"Saying her name. Stop saying her name. We agreed to keep it a surprise."

"I didn't say her name."

"You said her first initial."

"I gave her classification."

"When did she become an agent, anyway?"

"Super spy, to be exact."

"That's the life you want for her? A spy?"

"A *super* spy, Amy. And it's not the life I want for her. It's the life that chose her."

"I thought you wanted her to be a sports star."

"That too."

"Can someone be both?"

"There's that girl in the news who won the Spelling Bee and is really good at dribbling basketballs."

"I'm not sure that's the same thing."

"I don't actually care what she does with her life."

"I know."

"I just want her to carpe diem and all that."

"And all that."

"Seize the day."

"I know what it means."

"Make her life extraordinary."

"Are you literally quoting *Dead Poets Society* right now? Like, not just the carpe diem, but the rest of it too? You're even whispering like Robin Williams."

"I still want that, though."

"What?"

"Her life to be extraordinary."

"I'm sure she'll read her fair share of self-destructing messages. But first she and her mom need some rest."

"Mind if I keep my light on? I'm trying to find the chapter in this parenting book on how to teach your baby to walk away from an explosion without looking back. She'll never be a self-respecting super spy if she doesn't learn that."

Agent E

"No need for a light, Old Boots," she mutters to herself.

Didn't he know that eyes can adjust to the dark?

After six months in this crepuscular crevice—"a womb without a view," she snickers—Agent E can make out the cuticles on her itty-bitty nails.

Nails that will be perfect for untying knots while bound to a chair, should the need inevitably arise.

For now, she must wait. She must be patient. She must gather her strength.

Her mission, which she's already chosen to accept, commences in three months.

Did she really choose it, though?

Negatory.

Old Boots is right about that.

Her mission chose her.

Paul

"She lifted her head, man!"

"What?"

"Sorry. Gotta keep my voice down. Amy and the baby are sleeping. I'll go out in the hallway."

"The baby? She's here? Congrats, bro! You're a dad! How are they doing?"

"Both good. Both great. She lifted her head!"

"Who did?"

"The baby. You think I'd be calling you from the hospital to tell you Amy lifted her head?"

"No?"

"They're not supposed to be able to do that."

"What?"

"Lift their heads! The doctor said so. She said babies can't lift their heads yet. But she DID. After I handed her over to Amy. Lifted her head and looked right into Amy's eyes."

"Cool."

"That's all you have to say?"

"Really, really cool."

"You don't believe me, do you? My own brother doesn't believe me. That's okay—I'm used to it. The nurses don't believe me either. They nod and smile, but I can tell they're just humoring me. The doctor too."

"Didn't they witness the event?"

"No. Just me and Amy. I mean, they were there—we didn't have her on the way to the hospital or anything. But they weren't watching."

"They didn't watch when the baby arrived?"

"They saw the arrival, but not the meet 'n' greet.

"Heather just asked me to ask you how much the baby weighs and how long it is."

"How long it is?"

"She said it like it wasn't a weird question."

"Eight pounds, two ounces. Longer than a football."

"Heather doesn't look amused."

"Sorry. Longer than an *American* football. Was she thinking of an English football? Like, a soccer ball? Was that the confusion?"

"No, I don't think that's it—but it's good enough for me."

"You think I'm making up the head lifting?"

"No."

"Then why don't you sound impressed?"

"I guess I didn't know it was impressive."

"It is. It's impossible. That's what the doctor said."

"You told me. I'm just saying I didn't realize until now it was impossible."

"*Humanly* impossible. And my kid did it. That makes her superhuman."

"I'm a human. I can do it."

"Okay—*baby-ly* impossible. My wife gave birth to a super baby!"

"Heather wants to know the baby's name."

"Think I'm gonna stick with calling her Agent E."

"Quick. Turn off Amy's phone. Heather's texting her for more info right now. She's apparently willing to WAKE UP AMY to get it. Wait. Crisis averted. Heather came to her senses and put down the phone, but she doesn't look happy about it.

"Did you tell her that my daughter lifted her head? That might turn her frown upside down."

"Congrats on the super baby, bro."

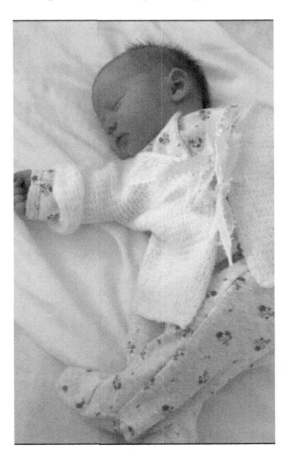

Agent E

The hospital room phone rings at a frequency only Agent E can detect. With painstaking surreption, she extricates herself from limbs and the receiver from its base.

"You lifted your head?!"

"A mistake, ma'am," she says, voice no more than a whisper yet enunciation unfailingly precise.

"What in blazes were you thinking?"

"An error of judgment, to be sure."

"Is your cover blown?!"

"Negatory, ma'am."

"What did the nurses say? The doctor?"

"Didn't see it. Don't believe it."

"We got lucky."

"Fortuitous indeed, ma'am."

"As long as I have you, shall we talk about the mission?"

"Negatory. Old Boots is on his way back to the room, ma'am."

"Old Boots?"

"My father, ma'am."

"Ah. Over and out."

"I wanted to see her face."

"Whose?"

"My mother's, ma'am."

"I see. Understandable. But we can't let sentimentality get in the way of the mission."

"A miscue on my part, ma'am. Won't happen again. Over and out."

"Over and out."

Paul

"Why is it tar?"

"What?"

"Her poop—why is it tar?"

"What are you talking about, Paul?"

"Sticky. Black. Tar, Amy."

"Should we get a nurse?"

"No, not tar. It's like that stuff the dinosaur spits on the guy—what's his name?"

"I don't know. Paul—"

"The fat guy—from *Seinfeld*."

"There are dinosaurs in *Seinfeld*?"

"No. *Jurassic Park*. Remember the dinosaur who spits that black, gunky, acid stuff onto that guy? Blinding him? Newman—that's his name in *Seinfeld*. I'm not sure what his name is in *Jurassic Park*."

"Would you like me to Google it?"

"Our baby just pooped black, gunky dinosaur spit, Amy."

"I'm calling a nurse. Oh, wait—here's one now. Perfect

timing. Hi. We have questions about our baby's poop. Also,

dinosaurs and the fat guy from *Jurassic Park*."

Agent E

"You put it where?"

"I'm open to alternative storage locations, ma'am, but the options appeared limited."

"That stuff is really sticky."

"Well aware of its viscosity, ma'am."

"It's designed to stop a fleeing target dead in their tracks. Splatter it on the floor, shoes stick to it, that sort of thing."

"It is indeed, as you say, sticky, ma'am."

"Was he able to remove the substance?"

"After much perseveration, Old Boots did persevere."

"And your flesh? Did it too persevere?"

"It was an abrasive experience, ma'am, but I remain tenderly intact."

"Has the threat of discovery been neutralized?"

"For the time being, ma'am."

"An operative?"

"Dressed as a nurse. She informed them that all babies' first bowel movements have similar properties. Even made up a fancy name for it: meconium."

"And they believed her?!"

"Affirmative, ma'am."

"Shall we debrief about your mission?"

"Truthfully, ma'am, I'm still recovering from the debriefing I just endured."

"Pun intended, I presume."

"Most definitely, ma'am."

"Well I'm bummed we can't keep talking. Get it? *Bummed*?"

"Alas, I do."

"No good?"

"Your wit knows no end, ma'am."

Paul

"It'll be good to get out of this hospital. Stretch our legs."

"I did plenty of stretching my legs right here in this hospital, Paul."

"Ha. You know what I mean."

"You mean you want to start looking for a new house? Because I'm not sure our two-and-a-half room apartment is as roomy as you make it sound."

"There's only two and a half of us. One room per person. It's perfect."

Paul

"Paul! PAUL!"

"Yes?"

"I could use a little help here!"

"Okay."

"The baby's going berserk. *I'm* going berserk. I can't find the milk bottle anywhere."

"They're in the washer."

"No—not all the milk bottles. Just this one. The one I was using just now. I know I left it somewhere in here."

"On top of your nightstand?"

"I thought so, but I don't see it. Maybe it fell. Could you get on your hands and knees and look under the bed?"

"It's not there."

"Could you all least try? I can't take any more of this screaming."

"I told you . . . It's in the washer."

"You put THAT one in the washer?"

"I put all of them in the washer."

"Including THAT one? That was our last bottle! The milk was still good!"

"I was just trying to help."

"WELL YOU DIDN'T HELP."

"Do I get any points for trying?"

"Sure. Imagine a basketball game. There are seconds left. You're down by one. You dribble the ball toward the basket, you shoot, you score. One problem: you scored on the wrong hoop. You were trying to help your team, but you helped the other team instead. And the scoreboard gives you credit for helping them instead of us."

"So our daughter is the other team?"

"Sure. But she's just doing her job."

"Whereas I'm . . . "

"Doing her job while on my team's payroll."

Paul

"If you ever become a father, remember to put men's t-shirts on the registry."

"Why?"

"Diapers, burp cloths, men's t-shirts."

"Same question, bro."

"I've run out of clean t-shirts."

"Because . . . you use them as burp cloths?"

"Ha."

"Or diapers?"

"I sweated through all of them in like two days."

"And so I say again: Why?"

"Because I don't have breasts."

"I don't think absence of breasts is why guys sweat more than women."

"Dude, those things are like tranquilizer darts for babies."

"What are?"

"Breasts. Without them, there's only one way to get babies back to sleep."

"Wringing your sweaty t-shirts out on them?"

"Walking and rocking. Simultaneously. We've got a rocking chair—no, we've got a rocker—"

"What's the difference between a rocking chair and a rocker?"

"One's sold at Toys 'R' Us."

"Gotcha."

"As far as I can tell, it's not for soothing an infant; it's for soothing a dad. The infant's still wailing away, but at least I can take a breather."

"From walking?"

"Exactly. I'm pretty sure there's actually grooves in our hardwood floors from my constant footsteps. The dining room, the kitchen, the living room. Around and around. Over and over."

"It's ironic, really."

"What?"

"The only two ways to soothe your kid are with breasts or by walking."

"Yeah."

"But by walking, you're ensuring you'll never have breasts."

"Is that a man boobs joke?"

"No good?"

"Not unless man boobs come loaded with milk."

"Fair enough."

"I'll trade a toned body for breasts with milk in them any day."

"You should tell Amy that."

"No, no I should not."

Agent E

"That's right, Old Boots," mutters Agent E. "Gulp as much oxygen as you need."

Her druthers were to work alone, of course, but performing feats of derring-do is not always a solo affair. The whole purpose of this mission, in fact, required collaboration.

"I'll get you whipped into shape one way or another."

Paul

"1914."

"What?"

"That's when the zipper was invented."

"Fun fact."

"Not fun at all, man. Deeply disturbing."

"Zippers are disturbing?"

"No, the lack of zippers is disturbing. Why in God's name do they make newborn clothing without zippers?"

"Zippers good. Noted."

"At first I thought maybe the non-zippered onesies people were giving us were hand-me-downs—maybe a generation ago zippers were nowhere to be found. Even if they were new clothes, I said to myself, maybe the older generation had just missed out on the newfangled zipper fad and didn't know any better. Like how my relatives always announce their name and the time when they leave a message, even though that info is already in our phones. But 1914? If zippers were invented in 1914 I have to believe they found their way into the public consciousness and onto baby clothes well before my daughter was born."

"Zippers blow away the competition, huh?"

"If you like successfully dressing a writhing, screaming infant in less than twenty minutes, then yes. If, on the other hand, you've always wanted to see what it's like to clasp a sheaf of loose-leaf paper into a three-ring binder while someone else tries to rip the binder out of your grasp, then clasps on newborn clothing are the way to go."

"Yikes."

"And don't even get me started on buttons. You ever have trouble buttoning the cuff of a dress shirt?"

"Yeah."

"It's like that, only you have to do it ten times and the baby is wailing at you the whole time like a nuclear plant siren in meltdown mode."

"I had no idea. Did the baby clothes we got you have zippers?"

"I don't remember, but you better hope so. I'm currently consulting with my lawyers. We're bringing a class action lawsuit. Total scorched earth. The clothing manufacturers, the stores, the customers that enable this senseless new parent abuse to continue: no one will be spared."

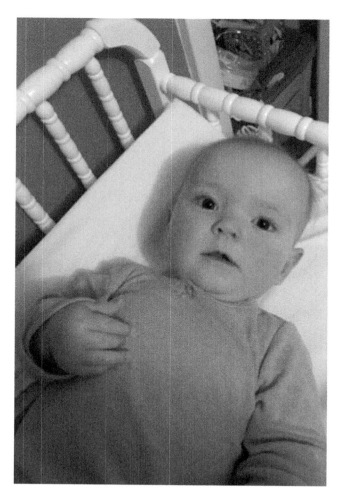

Paul

"Dude, what am I hearing?"

"I'll tell you what you're not hearing. My daughter crying."

"Awesome. So now will you tell me what that sound is?"

"Our treadmill. She stops crying instantly when I start it up."

"You put your infant on a treadmill? Doesn't she fall off? Or is this your way of telling me Agent E already knows how to walk?"

"I do the walking. She does the sleeping. That's the good news."

"There's bad news?"

"She wakes up and resumes wailing the second I step off the treadmill."

"So just keep walking forever and ever. Problem solved."

"I've been thinking of Sisyphus lately."

"I bet."

"Do you know why he had to push that boulder up the hill over and over for all eternity?"

"He was being punished, right?"

"So they say. My theory is that he had a kid strapped to his back who only slept when he engaged in backbreaking labor."

Paul

"Hey, Sisyphus. Still pushing boulders up a hill?"

"Pushing pacifiers into a mouth, mostly."

"Sounds less exhausting than the treadmill."

"Try doing it every three minutes for two days straight. Think I'm developing carpal tunnel."

"Pacifiers don't work?"

"Not when they're not in mouths they don't. You ever leave a coffee cup or something on the roof of your car?"

"Sure."

"Trying to keep a pacifier in a baby's mouth is like trying to drive on a highway without spilling that coffee. Actually, it's worse than that. Imagine the coffee cup needed to stay balanced on the roof for the car to work."

"Sounds like an adrenaline-fueled good time."

"Now imagine you're driving the car but haven't slept in two days."

"This is some analogy."

"Here's another one. Imagine you could only sleep if you watched yourself do it in front of a mirror. You needed to keep your eyes open in order to see yourself close your eyes."

"You really are sleep-deprived, aren't you?"

"That's what keeping a pacifier in a sleepy infant's mouth is like. You know it's working because they fall asleep. You know they fell asleep because they stopped sucking the pacifier, it fell out of their mouth, and now they're awake and screaming again."

"I'm still not following what that has to do with mirrors."

"You would if you hadn't slept in 48 hours."

"Idea: you know those birds that drink water?"

"Don't all birds drink water?"

"No—I mean, yes, but I'm talking about the things people have in their offices. They're wooden, I think? They keep going back and forth, like a lever, peck peck peck."

"Oh, yeah. People put a glass next to them and pretend they're drinking from it."

"Those are the ones. What if you set one of those next to

Agent E's mouth? It could peck the pacifier into place all night long."

"My brain might be sleep-deprived, but I know a GREAT idea

when I hear one."

"Done. I'll order one pronto."

Agent E

With her keen hearing, Agent E detects the susurrus of the stealthcopter's blades.

"Chopper's almost here, ma'am."

"Be prepared to hightail it when it arrives."

"I'll be ready, ma'am."

"You might even say you were born ready."

"Yes, ma'am."

"Do you see what I did there? You're a baby who's already a spy, so you literally were born ready."

"Affirmative."

"It's an expression."

"Indubitably, ma'am."

"And your parents? Are they taken care of?"

"Sleeping soundly."

"Are you sure they won't wake up?"

"I tuckered them out most profoundly, ma'am."

"And if they do wake up?"

"I looped the baby cam footage."

"Good thinking."

"They shall be none the wiser, ma'am."

"Thanks for agreeing to come in. Your mission gets more urgent by the day. Thought we better meet face to face."

"Rendezvous at HQ."

"Hey. That rhymes."

"Indubitably, ma'am."

Paul

"Can you turn off your phone, Paul? The screen is keeping me up."

"I'll turn it away from you."

"We should sleep when the baby's sleeping."

"What are we going to do?"

"About what?"

"About everything."

"You're doom scrolling again, aren't you?"

"Redundant. If I'm scrolling, I'm doom scrolling. There's no avoiding the doom."

"Sometimes I wish you still stayed up late watching sports."

"I do."

"Not as much as you stay up worrying about . . . "

"The downfall of humanity?"

"It'll be okay, Paul."

"How, Amy? How could we do this to our children? Grow up fast, kids! We torched this place and we need you to become firefighters! You won't have much time to put out the fire because you're just kids and we adults think the best way to stop conflagrations is to douse them with more flames. But when you grow up, maybe you can get rid of our flamethrowers and pick up a hose? Please and thank you."

"Wow. You came up with that speech on the spot?"

"It's my latest Facebook post. Not getting as many likes as I'd hoped."

"You asked me what we're going to do. What are *you* going to do?"

"I already wrote the Facebook post."

"Besides that."

"I don't know."

"Maybe you should figure that out. After getting some sleep."

"Yeah."

Agent E

"You're right, Old Boots," Agent E says, staring down at her house from her perch in the stealthcopter. (She's long since bugged all the rooms; she can hear their every comment, see their every movement. How else to keep tabs on them when she's away? How else to monitor their state of mind and body?) "We don't have time to wait for children to become adults."

Securing the rope around her waist, she goes airborne, noiselessly colliding with the house and rappelling down it, nimble fingers alacritously ajarring her bedroom window.

It's not until she's lying supine in her crib that she remembers the looped footage in the baby cam.

To anyone watching the monitor, she continues to serenely doze.

And it occurs to her that that might not be such a bad idea.

Her mission is far from over, of course.

It's just getting started.

But just because nefarious nemeses never nod off doesn't mean she can't either.

One super spy is nowhere near enough, she thinks—or starts

to. She's asleep before finishing the thought.

Paul

"Guhguhguhguhguh."

"What are you doing, Paul?"

"The nurse on the phone asked what the strange noises sounded like."

"Well she didn't sound like that."

"Yes she did."

"It was more like Gihgihgihgihgih."

"Did you hear that? Like, a clucking sound."

"You mean a clicking sound."

"No, I mean a clucking sound."

"Chickens cluck. You think our daughter sounded like a chicken?"

"Clucking doesn't only refer to chickens. It also means a sound like . . . like . . . "

"Clicking?"

"No, not clicking. I mean, yes—clicking but different. A deeper click. Do you understand what I'm saying, ma'am? Here, I'll try to make the sound again if—oh. Okay. Understood. Sorry for bothering you so late at night."

"What'd she say?"

"The clucking isn't something to worry about."

"What about clicking?"

"Either way, apparently."

"So all babies click?"

"Apparently."

"Apparently?"

"I mean, I didn't ask, but—"

"How could you not ask? Our baby sounds like she's trying to get a horse to gallop, and you're not curious if that's normal?"

"I think she sounds more like a turn signal."

"Oh. Great. That's much better. So long as I gave birth to a dashboard, there's nothing to worry about."

"Honestly, a turn signal might come in handy once she starts crawling."

"Ha. Isn't being new parents fun?"

"The funnest."

Agent E

"Morse code?"

"Morse code, ma'am."

"Sorry. Guess I was slow on the uptake."

"No mea culpa necessary, ma'am."

"What was the message?"

"Just a test, ma'am. Wondered if this might be another fruitful way you and I could communicate."

"Weren't you afraid your parents would freak out?"

"I figured they'd think I was making baby cooing noises, ma'am."

"That's what *I* thought you were doing."

"Yes, ma'am."

"It appears you gave me too much credit."

"I wouldn't put it that way, ma'am."

"And that you gave them too little."

"They didn't know it was Morse code, ma'am."

"Still."

"Still indeed, ma'am."

Paul

"Does it hurt when I do this?"

"No, doctor, it . . . YES."

"How about now?"

"Uh-huh."

"Now?"

"Aaaahhh."

"This?"

"Arrrrgghhhhhh."

"Okay—you can get down from there."

"What do you think is the problem?"

"You're getting old."

"I mean, is it muscular?"

"Most likely."

"The sore shoulder blades, the lower back, the leg—are they all connected?"

"Probably."

"I saw this show where a guy had pain in his left leg and it turned out to be bone cancer."

"It's not bone cancer, Mr. ..."

"Paul's fine. Should we at least do some x-rays?"

"I don't think there's any need for that, Paul."

"You're that sure of your diagnosis?"

"Pretty sure."

"What is it then?"

"You're getting old."

"You said that already. I mean, what's the medical term for it?"

"Getting old."

"So what do we do?"

"You said you've tried to stretch?"

"Yep."

"I can get you a referral for physical therapy."

"Where they'll have me do more stretches?"

"Pretty much."

"Will that help?"

"It can't hurt."

"That's not the same thing as helping."

"I mean, it *can* hurt. It *will* hurt. But it won't do any further damage."

"That's good, I guess."

"Just to clarify, there *will* be further damage. It just won't be because of the stretches, however much they hurt."

"What will do the damage?"

"Getting old."

"Limped right into that one."

Paul

"You ever tried lying on your back and kicking your legs non-stop for hours at a time?"

"Is that what you're doing now, man? You sound out of breath."

"I can only last a matter of minutes."

"Lasted long enough to create your daughter, wink wink."

"She keeps kicking for like an hour straight, maybe two. If there was ever a doubt Agent E's a super agent, this confirms it. Her stamina is off the charts."

"Sounds incredible, bro."

"It's exhilarating. And boring."

"Ha. Really?"

"Remember watching *Jurassic Park*?"

"You already told me about her dinosaur spit poop."

"No, I mean the first time. Do you remember watching *Jurassic Park* the first time, in the theater?"

"Yeah. We went together. Got there late and had to sit in front. I remember having to crane my neck to see the dinosaurs."

"Me, too. Do you remember the first dinosaurs you get to see?"

"Maybe?"

"There's a scary dino eye or something at the very beginning, but the first time you see a whole dinosaur is the brontosauruses."

"Aren't they called brachiosauruses now?"

"Whatever. The giraffe dinosaur."

"Right."

"Only they weren't giraffes. They were real dinosaurs. The music is swelling—da na nah na na, da na nah na na—and there are real dinosaurs. That's what it looked like—remember?"

"I definitely remember it being cool."

"Mind-blowing. But imagine if that was the whole movie. Real long-necked dinosaurs chewing on branches."

"Short movie."

"No. I mean, what if *Jurassic Park* had been two hours of watching long-necked dinosaurs munching on foliage. That two hours would have felt like two days, no matter how real or long their necks were. It would still have been mind-blowing—REAL ACTUAL dinosaurs! But it would also have been mind-*numbing*."

"For sure."

"That's parenting an infant. She's moving at, like, an astonishing rate. But she's also not going anywhere. She's just lying there. Don't get me wrong. It's miraculous. It's jaw-dropping. And it's so, so boring."

"I better let you go, bro. You sound winded. You're actually wheezing."

Paul

"Doomscrolling again?"

"As a matter of fact, Amy, I'm getting involved like we talked about."

"Registering to help at a protest?"

"No."

"Signing up to do some phone banking?"

"Nope."

"Buying a yard sign?"

"Nah-ah."

"Then . . . Paul."

"Amy?"

"You're on Facebook again."

"It's not what it looks like."

"You said you were going to do something *other* than post on Facebook."

"I *am*."

"How?"

"I'm not posting, Amy—I'm commenting on someone else's post."

"You're a true activist."

"It's going to work this time. I'm going to show this guy the light. Rational, compassionate, passionate discussion will win out, restoring my—nay, our, *all* of our—trust in democracy."

"Goodnight, Paul."

"When the cock crows tomorrow he will be calling forth a new dawn in our democratic republic."

"I think the cocks are doing plenty of crowing already."

Paul

"I think our marriage is on the rocks."

"Really, bro?"

"Yesterday we went to the beach."

"You mean your marriage is on the sand."

"Ha."

"Can a marriage be on the rocks when you're at a beach?"

"It was after that. When we got home."

"I'm listening."

"She carried the baby upstairs to her crib, while I got the stuff from the car."

"What stuff?"

"Towels, cooler, sunblock. I set it all down when I got inside. I was going to take it downstairs but I figured I'd better take off my shoes first. Amy hates it when I wear shoes around the house."

"Look at you being all thoughtful."

"Right? That's when I noticed all the dirty dishes."

"You made a barefooted beeline for them?"

"Sure did."

"What a guy."

"That's what I was thinking. Amy's going to come into the kitchen and see my what-a-guy-ness."

"Didn't happen?"

"First thing she says is: 'Are you crazy? You woke up the baby with all that clanging.'"

"Oops."

"Second thing she says is: 'I thought you said you were going to put away the towels and stuff.'"

"Oh. Right. Forgot about those."

"Third thing she says is: 'You didn't even use a towel to wipe off your feet? You're tracking sand all over the kitchen.'"

"Sure."

"Fourth thing she says is: 'Where's my water bottle? Did you put it in the dishwasher?'"

"Perfect."

"She asked me how I could pick up the bottle and not realize it was still cold and she was in the middle of explaining how said bottle was irreplaceable because the ice had melted just right when the baby started crying and gave me an excuse to get the hell out of there."

"Was the baby at least grateful for your what-a-guyness?"

"I never made it out of the kitchen. Amy yelled at me about how I was going to leave sand all over the house. She tossed me a towel from the pile on the floor as she ran to the baby."

"Of course. You two actually on the rocks?"

"Nah."

"Good. I mean, she does have a point."

"Yeah."

"About the ice especially. There is an optimal meltedness."

"No argument here."

Paul

"My daughter is punking me."

"When you say she's punking you..."

"Pranking me. Playing me for a fool."

"Your baby daughter is . . ."

"Pulling a fast one."

"How old is she?"

"Eight months."

"And she's outsmarting you."

"She WAS outsmarting me—but not anymore. I'm onto her little gambit."

"Are you going to tell me, bro, or...."

"She keeps pretending she can't crawl."

"Pretending?"

"For weeks now."

"So you spied her actually crawling?"

"Might as well have. It's so obvious, now that I think about it."

"What is?"

"Her ruse. Every time I set her on her belly, she gets up on all fours. And I'm like, 'Okay, here we go—my kid's about to motor around the room, full steam ahead.' She's in fundamentally sound position. All she has to do is lift a knee cap or a hand and she's off to the races. Honestly, it'd be easier to crawl than not to crawl."

"That's awesome."

"I swear, sometimes I even see her leg twitch. But then, just as I know this is it, this is the moment we've all been waiting for, she flops on her belly and starts kicking her legs and arms wildly like she can swim through the air or something."

"Sounds like she's really close, bro."

"That's what I thought. But I'm not falling for it again. The scales have dropped from my eyes."

"The what?"

"It's an expression."

"Are you sure?"

"Positive."

"If you say so."

"I do say so. The kid's a con artist. And, really, not a very good one. She's like one of those people who pretends to have broken their leg after getting bumped by a car, but then crutches into court on the wrong leg."

"Now your kid's an ambulance chaser?"

"No. An ambulance chaser is the lawyer. My kid's already in the ambulance, telling everyone her vocal cords were damaged in the accident and she can't talk."

"Ah."

"WHILE TALKING."

"Yeah, got that."

"Nice try, kid. But you'll have to do better than that if you want to take me for a ride."

"On the ambulance?"

"No. It's an expression."

"If you say so."

Paul

"How's dadding going, bro?"

"Good."

"Nice."

"Over the last couple hours I've terrified and permanently emotionally scarred my eight-month-old daughter. Oh, and I've royally pissed off my wife."

"But other than that . . . good?"

"Exactly."

"You wanna talk about it?"

"Striking terror into the heart of my baby or enraging the mother of said infant daughter?"

"Something tells me they're related."

"Something is a reliable source."

"That silence you hear is me waiting for you to go on."

"It all started a long time ago in a galaxy far, far away."

"What does this have to do with *Star Wars*?"

"I watched it today. Turns out Darth Vader scares her."

"You watched *Star Wars* with your daughter?"

"I didn't mean to."

"You didn't know she was there?"

"Yeah. I knew. But she's only eight months. The way I figure it, I have an ever-closing window to watch whatever I want. Then it's going to be like ten straight years of kids' movies."

"Whatever you want?"

"She's not really aware of me watching yet, you know? I make sure I'm holding her so her face is over my shoulder, away from the screen, because screens are bad for babies."

"And then you watch, like, *Terminator* or *Kill Bill*?"

"Today it was *Star Wars*."

"Featuring Darth Vader."

"Not sure why she turned her head and looked at the screen. Maybe it was Darth's breathing. Whatever the reason, she lifted her head from my shoulder and swiveled it to the TV—just in time to see the smoke evaporate and Darth come marching down the white corridor toward the camera."

"Toward your daughter."

"Exactly."

"Freaked her out?"

"She lost it. Screamed bloody murder. Wouldn't stop."

"Enter your wife?"

"We tried everything. We rocked her. I walked her. She nursed her."

"Nothing worked?"

"And the whole time nothing was working, Amy was looking at the TV screen. Her face was boiling just like our kid's."

"And so you apologized, said you clearly made a mistake, turned off the TV."

"I went for a run."

"Today?"

"I needed to get out of the house."

"It was like negative 40 degrees today."

"The air stabbed my lungs."

"Heard on the radio it was the coldest day in years."

"Blurred my eyes with tears, then froze those tears."

"So . . . ?"

"I needed to get out of there. The kid was still shrieking. My wife was still boiling. I needed to go outside in the cold so my kid and wife could cool down inside."

"Did you just come up with that?"

"I've been re-telling the story in my head all day. Anyway. Before I left for the run, I put on my jacket, my gloves, my hat . . . and my face mask. My black face mask."

"Oh no."

"Yep. Because I'm a genius, I returned from my run in my black mask and breathing loudly. White steam poured out of my mask with every breath."

"Don't tell me, bro."

"I open the door right as my kid is dragging herself along the floor, like ten feet away. She's not crying. There are salt streaks down her cheeks but no new tears. Somehow, Amy must've finally soothed her. I don't know if it's my breathing, or the freezing blast of air from the door, or what. But the kid swivels her head, looks up. And she sees a dude in a black mask, steam billowing, breathing loudly."

"Loses it again?"

"Instant tears. But that's not the worst part."

"It's not?"

"Nope. The worst part is—genius that I continue to be—I don't get it. I've forgotten I'm wearing a mask. So I march forward to give her a hug and console her. Just like Vader marched at her in the movie. Her shrieks were blood-curdling."

"Please, please don't tell me you told her you were her father."

"Oh, God. Come to think of it..."

Paul

"Hey, bro."

"Chuck Yeager breaking the sound barrier."

"What about it?"

"Legendary ballplayer Cool Papa Bell being so fast he'd flip his bedroom switch and be in bed before the light went out."

"Did you butt-dial me?"

"Usain Bolt delivering Jimmy John's."

"Usain Bolt doing what? Oh, wait. You're monologuing. Is that it?"

"In the annals of speed, another entry must be logged: At 4:36 in the afternoon, one Paul Hoblin realized the library closed at 5:00. He had 16 almost-overdue picture books to track down and a baby to persuade into a jacket, a hat, two shoes, and a car seat. Future generations will read of Hoblin's feat of derring-do and assume they're being regaled by a tall tale, a myth, a parable of hyperbolic proportions. But the simple-yet-impossible fact is that Hoblin returned from the library at 5:03, books returned, baby fully clothed, and with a new stack of books in hand.

No word on whether he arrived staggering from the G-forces he must have experienced during his light-speed adventures."

"You wrote that down, right? You were reading from a script."

"A Facebook post."

"Should've known. Still...."

"What?"

"That one wasn't all doom and gloom."

"The republic needs inspiration to fend off expiration."

"Ah. Is that what it needs?"

"You don't sound inspired."

"Good job with the books, man."

"Are you mocking me?"

"Top-notch dadding, dude."

"Damn right it was."

Paul

"Bro."

"My kid is playing psychological mind games on me."

"Mind games?"

"Psychological mind games."

"Isn't that redundant?"

"Whatever. What I—"

"Psychology is the study of the mind, so it goes without saying that mind games are psy"—

"WHAT I'M TRYING TO SAY is that she's torturing me through mental manipulation."

"Yeah?"

"Yeah. About an hour ago she came stumbling up to me, giggled, and handed me one of her books."

"Sounds . . . awful?"

"It was great. I took the book, opened it, and . . . she went full banshee."

"Full banshee?"

"Blood-curdling screams. Followed by full-bodied sobbing."

"What did you do?"

"I closed the book."

"Good call."

"You'd think so, but nope. She somehow managed to wail even louder."

"Maybe it wasn't about the book?"

"That's what I thought, so I set the book down."

"No good?"

"She marched over to the book, still screaming, picked it up, and dropped it in my lap again."

"So you . . . "

"Opened the book again."

"And she . . ."

"Lost her shit again. This time she actually ripped the book out of my hands and chucked it across the room."

"Problem solved?"

"Ha. She hustled across the room, scooped up the book, and brought it back to me."

"So what did you do?"

"Everything I could think of. I opened and closed the book and pretended it could talk. I wore the book as a hat. I tore off a corner of a page and ate it."

"You ate a page?"

"I would have. But my chewing just made her more upset. So I spit it out and taped it back in the book."

"What finally worked?"

"Worked?"

"I don't hear her screaming now."

"That's because I'm not in the house. I'm in the garage, contemplating my own sanity."

"You didn't, like, stick a tennis ball in the exhaust, did you?"

"Not yet. But I swear, it's like I can still hear her screams through the walls."

"Oh. Wait. I hear them too. You're not hearing voices. I mean, you are. But they're real."

"Now do you believe me? I'm the target of a psyop operation."

"Isn't that redundant? Psyop stands for psychological operation, right? So it doesn't make sense to say a psychological operation operation. Bro? You there? What are you doing?"

"Looking for a tennis ball."

Agent E

"Is that what you're doing, Agent? Playing mind games with him?"

"I wouldn't put it that way, ma'am."

"Well how would you put it?"

"These are the times that try men's souls. The summer soldier and the sunshine patriot will, in this crisis, shrink from the service of their country; but he that stands by it now, deserves the love and thanks of man and woman."

"Your words?"

"Thomas Paine's, ma'am."

"Ah. And is that what you're trying to do? Pain him? Try his soul?"

"No matter how desperate we are that someday a better self will emerge, with each flicker of the candles . . . we know it's not to be—that for the rest of our sad, wretched, pathetic lives, this is who we are to the bitter end. Inevitably, irrevocably."

"Yikes. That's what you want him to learn? Talk about bleak. Who was that? Thomas Paine again?"

"Jerry Seinfeld, ma'am. Season 4, episode 15."

Paul

"I'm overtired."

"I bet, bro."

"That's the word I keep hearing. Overtired. But isn't that redundant? If you're tired, you're already . . . well, tired. Nobody says they're the right amount of tired, do they?"

"I think they just mean so tired you can't function."

"I'm definitely that."

"Yeah?"

"Delirious is probably a better word. This morning I walk into the play room and the baby is on the phone."

"The phone?"

"Not the real phone, obviously. Not even her toy phone. She's holding a plastic banana to her ear."

"Love it."

"That's what I thought. She's speaking gibberish, of course. But she's saying the words so matter-of-factly."

"The non-words."

"The gibberish, yeah. I'm telling you: the cadence of her voice was so realistic. She was even pausing to listen to whoever was on the other end of the line."

"Impressive."

"And it got to the point where . . ."

"Where?"

"Where I started to suspect there really was someone on the other end."

"I think you're overtired, brother."

"It gets worse. She was facing away from me. I was pretty sure she hadn't seen me. So I start creeping toward her on the tips of my toes. When I get above her, I crouch down real fast and swipe the phone—"

"The banana."

"The banana. I swipe the banana from her hands and ear and bring it up to my own."

"And you hear . . . a mysterious voice?"

"Nope."

"A voice you recognize?"

"No voice."

"Go figure."

"Don't laugh. It's worse."

"Worse how?"

"I hear a dial tone."

"Say what?"

"The baby's screaming her head off—I just scared her and took her toy—but I swear to God, even with her making it impossible to hear almost anything else, I thought I could make out a faint buzzzzzz."

"From the banana."

"Told you. I'm losing it."

"I'm sure you're fine."

"You don't sound sure."

"Might be a good idea to sit the next few plays out."

"Agreed."

Agent E

"Thank God you were speaking in code, Agent."

"And that he doesn't know Tolkien's Elvish, ma'am."

"How could you let him sneak up on you like that?"

"He may not speak their language, but apparently his feet are as light as elves', ma'am."

Paul

"She said her first word!"

"Really?! Was it 'Mom'?"

"Nope."

"'Mama'?"

"That's the same thing. And still no."

"Look at you grinning and satisfied with yourself. It was 'Dad', wasn't it?"

"'Barnacle.'"

"What?"

"Her first word was *barnacle*."

"Jesus, Paul."

"What? I'm serious."

"You get why this is mean, right? Like, haha and all that, but you realize I actually *did* think you were serious, right?"

"I was, Amy. I *am*."

"I just don't think it's very nice."

"I was giving her a bath. I kept pointing to myself and saying, 'Dad. Dad. Who am I?' But instead of saying *Dad*, she said *barnacle*."

"Fine, Paul. You're a barnacle. Is that what you want me to say?"

"No, that's not what I want you to say. That's what *she* said. Barnacle. Clear as day."

"You win."

"I'm not trying to win. What are you doing?"

"Calling my mom."

"Remind me again how this is me winning? How is you complaining about me to your mom me winning?"

"I'm not calling to complain. I'm calling to lament."

"Oh. My mistake. That's much better."

"I know you didn't mean anything. But that doesn't mean it didn't hurt my feelings. I was excited, Paul. I know you get that."

"I'm excited too!"

"Hi, Mom. Yes, I'm fine. It's nothing. It's just, Paul said something—he came in here and—"

"SHE SAID BARNACLE AMY I SWEAR."

Agent E

Agent E sighs, screws up her courage, answers the phone.

"Hello, ma'am. Before you say—"

"*Barnacle?* You said *barnacle?* Or was it some Elvish word that sounds like barnacle?"

"I lost my cool, ma'am."

"Is that why you did it? To look cool?"

"I got fed up, ma'am."

"Fed up? Weren't you taking a bath? Who gets fed up lounging in warm water?"

"It was patronizing, ma'am."

"What? Getting bathed? You knew that was part of the mission. You're okay pooping your pants and letting someone wipe your butt for you, but getting a spa day is infantilizing? You're an infant--of course you're going to be infantilized!"

"I don't disagree, ma'am. It's not the wiping nor the bathing that tries my soul. It's the language acquisition."

"The language acquisition?"

"Dad, dad, dad, dad. And then having the gall to ask, 'Who am I?' You've been telling me you're the paterfamilias ad nauseum for weeks, Old Boots; quit acting like you're giving me a pop quiz."

"I see you're calling him Old Boots again."

"If the name fits, ma'am."

"Won't call him Dad when he's in or out of earshot—is that it?"

"At least I didn't call him *cretin*, ma'am."

"No, just *barnacle*."

"I don't believe he took the word as a personal epithet."

"How *did* you come up with the word, anyway?"

"Ma'am?"

"Seems pretty random."

"There was a toy boat adrift in the tub, ma'am."

"Ah. So why didn't you just say *boat*. A lot less risky, no?"

"No, ma'am. I don't believe so. *Boat* is believable. *Barnacle* strains credulity. No one will believe him when he tells them what I said."

"I don't get it."

"I wanted my mother to hear what she thinks is my first word, ma'am."

"Understandable. In that case, quick thinking."

"Thank you, ma'am."

"For someone who wasn't thinking, I mean."

"Indubitably, ma'am."

"Over and out, Agent Barnacle."

"Over and out."

Agent E sighs again. Disaster, as ever, has been narrowly averted. The fallout, as ever, remains to be seen.

She could use a little bed time reading. Calm her nerves. Quiet the thumping in her ears.

She reaches under her crib mattress, practiced fingers searching for the slit in the fabric.

Pulls out a well-thumbed copy of *Moby Dick* and picks up where she left off.

Paul

"I signed a petition!"

"Cool. For what?"

"It doesn't matter."

"It doesn't?"

"I mean, it matters. Of course it does. But what really matters is that I signed it."

"Okay. Cool, bro."

"And I was holding my daughter when I did it. That's probably actually *why* I did it. If it wasn't for her, I would have made up some excuse, let my voice trail and shut the door. But I didn't want her to see that. I want her to see her father as someone who commits himself to causes, you know? All my life, I've claimed to have strong opinions. I've claimed to believe in stuff."

"You? Strong opinions? I've only heard your rant against instant replay in sports two or three hundred times."

"But do I go to the protest?"

"Honestly, I think it would be a pretty poorly attended protest. Who other than you is against instant replay?"

"Do I write my Congressperson?"

"A letter to the commissioners of various sports leagues might make more sense."

"Do I do anything other than rant and rave?"

"You *are* a pretty good ranter, though."

"True."

"Not a bad raver, either."

"I signed on the dotted line, man!"

"Nice, dude."

"Next up, yard signs."

"Can at least one of them be about instant replay?"

"Obviously."

"Did you give Agent E all the credit?"

"You know it. Told her I did it for her. Honestly, I'm starting to get the impression that she's the one training *me* and not the other way around."

"Sounds about right. How did she respond?"

"Smirked knowingly. She either knew exactly what I was saying or she was pooping."

"Maybe both."

Agent E

"How'd he figure it out?"

"Hard to say, ma'am."

"Is your cover blown?"

"Not deleteriously so."

"What, exactly, does he know?"

"My father knows fleetingly little, ma'am."

"You didn't call him Old Boots."

"An oversight, ma'am."

"You called him your father."

"I suppose he is indeed one and the same."

"Has it dawned on him that he's your mission?"

"The particulars of my work remain well beyond his grasp."

"Quick thinking pooping your pants."

"I'd rather not dwell on that, if it's all the same to you."

"Really threw him off the scent, if you know what I mean."

"Regrettably, I do, ma'am."

"Well, carry on then."

"Boats against the current, ma'am."

"Literary reference?"

"Indubitably, ma'am."

"InDOODYbly! You gotta admit—that one was good, right?"

Paul & Agent E

"You did it! You made your first basketball shot!" Paul says, doing a dance around the mini plastic hoop.

Agent E observes her father's enthusiastic antics, both bemused and strangely buoyed by them.

She watches him shoot a shot of his own.

You made it, too, she thinks.

We made it.

So far.

We have a long way to go, but so far we've both made it.

Paul

"My kid is colorblind."

"What?"

"It's okay. It's fine. It's not the end of the world."

"Right, but—"

"She can still live a full life."

"Of course she can, bro. But—"

"It's best to come to terms with it now, so we don't have to do it later."

"We?"

"Amy and I. She's currently in denial."

"She doesn't think your kid is colorblind?"

"There's nothing to think. It's not about thinking. The evidence is in. She can't tell a yellow crayon from a blue one, a green one from a pink one. I tried to play Connect Four with her, but it was hopeless because she couldn't distinguish red from black."

"And that's not normal?"

"Being colorblind is perfectly normal. Remember Mr. Johansen?"

"Our teacher from elementary school."

"He was colorblind."

"He was?"

"He told us he had to memorize where the red light and green light were located at intersections, but other than that, he lived a totally normal life."

"Cool. I was just—"

"She won't be able to see a rainbow, I suppose."

"Of course she'll be able to see it."

"Exactly. Good clarification. She just won't be able to see the colors. Maybe you should talk to Amy. Talk some sense into her. Tell her that gray rainbows can still have a pot of gold at the end of them."

"Sorry, bro. That doesn't sound like something I'd ever say."

Agent E

"What's the strategy here, Agent?"

"Ma'am?"

"The colorblindness. Why the ruse?"

"Verisimilitude, ma'am."

"Come again?"

"According to my research, babies typically cannot verbally distinguish colors, often until they are three years old."

"Seriously?"

"So says Wikipedia, ma'am."

"And that's all that this is about? You're not doing this to torment your father?"

"He says himself that me being colorblind is perfectly fine, ma'am."

"Uh-huh. That's what I thought."

"Ma'am?"

"Just remember: your job isn't to put him through the ringer. Your job is to get him off his keyster."

"I don't believe the two are mutually exclusive, ma'am."

"Maybe not always. But then again maybe sometimes."

"He could do the same research I'm doing, ma'am."

"Maybe you could show him that, Agent."

Paul

"I think my kid is going to be a zoologist."

"I thought she was going to be a secret agent."

"She IS a secret agent. But she'll need a cover story."

"True. What's a zoologist?"

"Someone who works in a zoo, I think."

"I don't think that's quite right, bro."

"Well it's what I mean when I say zoologist."

"I take it the zoo went well?"

"She spent the whole time naming the animals."

"Think that's taxonomy—not zoology."

"You mean taxidermy?"

"No—that's dead animals."

"Why do dead animals need to hire someone to do their taxes?"

"Ha. You were saying? Naming animals?"

"Right. She was really good at it. If by really good you mean she called every animal a dog."

"Efficient. Simple."

"'DOG,' she'd say, pointing at a lion or penguin or snake."

"Did you try to correct her?"

"Sometimes. No, I'd tell her, that's a mongoose. She'd keep pointing and say, 'DOG' again. Like she was helping me learn to pronounce it."

"Classic zoologist behavior."

"One time Amy and I spotted a seal. It was hard to see. We were at the bottom of the tank and the seal was at the top and off in one corner. We had to tilt our heads to get a good look at it. Look, we said to our daughter, a SEAL! We both pointed, but she didn't respond. We tapped the glass. We crouched down to see if it was even possible to spot the damn thing from her vantage point. As we were crouching, she said, 'DOG' again. And we were like yes, yes, dog. You see it! Then we turned around, expecting her neck to be craned and her finger to be pointing."

"Her finger wasn't pointing?"

"It was, but not at the seal. Not even at the tank. She was pointing at a seeing eye dog standing a few feet from us."

"It really was a dog!"

"Yep. Even a broken clock...."

"What does someone who needs a seeing eye dog do at a zoo, anyway?"

"No idea. Maybe he's a zoologist too."

Paul

"Paul? Paul!"

"Hmmmmm?"

"What are you reading? Hello, Earth to Paul."

"What?"

"You're reading . . . a romance novel?"

"No. I'm reading a *trashy* romance novel."

"Where'd you find it?"

"A bookstore. Did you know there's a whole section of books like this?"

"You didn't?"

"I had an inkling. It's not like in those old rental movie stories where there was a curtain separating this section from the rest."

"You mean the pornography section? You're saying this book is pornography?"

"No. It's way more illicit than pornography."

"My grandmother used to read those."

"Exactly. And did she ever talk out loud about what's in them?"

"You're saying *my grandmother* was no better than some teenage boy with a stack of *Playboys* under his bed?"

"No. I'm saying that your grandmother was wayyyyy better than that teenage boy. She somehow managed to get her freak on without having to hide it. Imagine it: millions of little old church ladies reading this smut with no judgment whatsoever. Hell, they might even complain about naughty words kids say these days, then go home and consume some real naughty words."

"Is it really that explicit?"

"It's more than explicit. It's a fully immersive experience. Videos don't let you know what the characters are thinking."

"How did you . . . ?"

"Break the code? Discover the matrix? Remember a few weeks ago when we were watching that show, and it started to get good, and right then the kid woke up and I had to go check on her?"

"I remember."

"And remember how every time we're in here, and it starts to get good, the kid wakes up so we have to stop and go check on her?"

"I REMEMBER."

"It got me thinking: How do other parents do it? How does it get good without waking up the kid?"

"This is the first time you've thought of that?"

"It's the first time I came up with an answer that wasn't just, 'I guess their kids must be deeper sleepers.'"

"Romance novels?"

"Not at first. I was trying to find the screenplay for that show we were watching."

"You were?"

"Sure. What better way to finish the scene without anyone hearing it? No luck, though. The Google Machine didn't seem to have it. But it turns out the show is based on a book. That's what got me in the bookstore."

"I think I'm impressed with you right now."

"If you're impressed now, wait 16 years. I've learned some stuff to show you."

"Sixteen years?"

"That's when our daughter will have moved out of the house. We won't have to worry about waking her up."

Paul

"Amy didn't know Mountain Dew shrinks your dick."

"My dick?"

"Dicks generally. Remember that rumor? From when we were kids?"

"Oh yeah . . . it was some ingredient, right?"

"Dye Yellow 5."

"Just had a flashback. Jeremy? No, Jordy. Jordy Lindstrom swatting a can of Sunkist Lemonade out of my hand like it was poisoned."

"I wonder if the kids who believed the Yellow 5 rumors back then are the adults who believe in conspiracy theories today."

"You should have your secret agent daughter infiltrate the groups spreading conspiracies. She can ask them, all casual-like, if they want to drink Mountain Dew."

"Are you mocking me?"

"No way."

"Are you pointing out that I'm making fun of people who believe in conspiracies while simultaneously believing my infant daughter is a secret agent?"

"The thought hadn't even occurred to me."

"Because that's totally different."

"Totally."

"My daughter really is a super spy."

"I couldn't agree more."

Agent E

"Maybe your dad is onto something here, Agent."

"Ma'am?"

"A lot of the conspiracy theorists ARE men."

"Ergo . . ."

"Maybe they think the government is force-feeding them Yellow 5?"

"The Deep State is preventing them from going deep, ma'am?"

"Ha."

"Going after their university's endowment?"

"Bingo."

"Gives a whole new meaning to the accusation that colleges lean left, ma'am."

"PRIVATE SCHOOLS."

"Precisely, ma'am."

"Liberal InDICKtrination."

"Subtle as always, ma'am."

"Should I put an agent on the case?"

"Or Freud."

"A psychiatrist?"

"A shrink, ma'am."

Paul

"I think I'm a truckist."

"A truckist, bro?"

"It's like a racist or a sexist, except it's not about race or gender. It's about truck drivers."

"You discriminate against truck drivers?"

"I instinctually assume the worst about them."

"Where do you think these feelings come from?"

"Experience. Firsthand experience."

"Did a truck driver do something to you?"

"Are you kidding me? It's practically a daily occurrence. On snowy or icy days, it's always trucks who barrel down the road as though the conditions are top-notch. They ride my bumper like they're drafting me, then they whoosh by me, their tires churning through the road slush and splattering it against my windshield."

"Sounds really traumatic."

"Are you telling me you've never noticed the preponderance of dickheads in trucks? Just the other day I was sitting in bumper to bumper traffic and it happened again."

"It?"

"We're all just inching along, when a truck driver gets impatient, swerves into the side of the road and cruises past all of us, like they're a VIP going through their own special metal detector while the rest of us have to shuffle along in an endless cordoned-off zig-zag."

"Maybe what you really are is a budgerist."

"A budgerist?"

"Someone who hates people who budge in lines—on the road, in the airport, wherever."

"I'm definitely a budgerist, but aren't we all? I feel like my antipathy for truck drivers goes beyond my general disdain for budgers. Like, you know what happens when trucks blaze by me on the side of the road?"

"What?"

"I daydream then and there about a police car, sirens blaring, following the truck in hot pursuit."

"Justice being served."

"If it was just that I wouldn't feel so alarmed. But what I'm hoping for isn't justice. It's vengeance."

"Vengeance? What did they ever do to you?"

"I don't know, exactly. That's what makes me a truckist. I irrationally assume they're all out to get me personally."

"Maybe you secretly want to be them?"

"What do you mean?"

"Like homophobes who are actually gay. Maybe you secretly *are* a trucker, if you only had the courage to live your authentic life. Maybe you're a road rebel stuck in a rule-follower's body."

Paul

"What are you looking for, Paul?"

"Whiskey."

"Tough day?"

"Tough career."

"They still have you organizing files all day?"

"I wish."

"What now?"

"I spent the day writing loan rejection letters."

"Ouch."

"To Whom It May Concern: You know how you have a dream? After careful review, I have decided to crush it."

"Maybe it's for their own good? Maybe you're saving them from future bankruptcy?"

"You sound like my boss."

"So what are you going to do about it?"

"About your spot-on impression of Gary?"

"About your soul getting sucked out."

"Did you not hear that I was looking for whiskey?"

"So that's your plan? Come home every day and make a beeline for the liquor cabinet?"

"You got a better idea?"

"Leave your job?"

"In this economy?"

"Paul."

"Amy."

"You're not trapped. You don't have to do something you don't want to do."

"No, I have to do something I chose to do. I don't know how my parents convinced me to get a major in Finance along with my English degree, but I guess they were right."

"They were?"

"Sure. My double major makes me perfect for writing these rejections. Gary said I'd finally found my niche."

"So the plan is to be miserable, then drown your sorrows in alcohol."

"Sorrows? This is a celebration."

"For what, exactly?"

"Job security."

"I hate when you act helpless like this."

"Not helpless. Hopeless."

"In that case, cheers for giving up?"

"Bottom's up!"

Paul

"You wanna watch the game on Sunday? Amy and the kid are gonna be at her mom's."

"Sweet. Wing World?"

"Can't. Wing World banned me from their premises."

"Bro. WHAT."

"Pretty sure part of staff training now includes practice spotting me, no matter what alias or fake mustache I'm wearing."

"How have you never told me this?"

"It's not a story I'm proud of."

"Even better. I'm all ears."

"About a year ago—two? It was before the kid. I was there with a big group."

"Thanks for the invite."

"It was with work friends—and I use that term lightly. Imagine air quotes around 'friends.' I was still fairly new at my job, and I was trying to convince myself and them that I fit in. Did you know bankers could be really into soccer?"

"I mean, in other parts of the world. In America, I thought you had to be a hippie or a hipster."

"Me too. But here we all were. In suits and ties in the middle of the day, and I swear, all of their eyes were glued to the TV. They were cheering for things that weren't goals—so they must have been true fans."

"How do you get banned from a restaurant when you're in a suit and tie with your co-workers?"

"I'm getting to that. The beers hadn't arrived. We'd been there a while, and all we'd ordered was beer, no food. For some reason, our waiter was nowhere to be found. Maybe they were short staffed that day. My co-workers had started to notice. And I had an idea."

"Uh-oh."

"Agreed. Never a good idea for me to have a good idea."

"What did you do?"

"Remember in high school when we would all end up at Benny's because they were open all night?"

"Can't beat Benny's."

"And how the food was always late and cold?"

"Could never figure that out. I get how with only one cook at night the food would be slow. But cold too?"

"Agreed. This one time, Tyler Erickson was with us. He wasn't usually. He wasn't really part of the group. If anything, he was too cool for us."

"Speak for yourself."

"As we were all sitting there, complaining about how long we'd been waiting for our orders, Tyler gets up and makes a beeline for the kitchen. He comes back out with a tray carrying all our food."

"Oh, yeah! I remember that."

"Dude was a hero that night. I didn't tell anyone, but I was in awe of him. The rest of us had just sat there countless nights, but Tyler was a man of action. I wanted to be just like him when I grew up."

"I think I see where this is going."

"Here was my chance, I realized. A whole table of people waiting for their drinks, just as helpless as we were back at Benny's. And I knew just what to do. I was going to save the day. 'I got this,' I told them."

"You went into the kitchen? That's how you got kicked out? I have to say, I'm kind of impressed."

"Hold your applause. I did go into the kitchen. But I didn't get caught—not yet. There, on a counter, was a tray loaded with drinks. It was so loaded, in fact, I wasn't exactly sure how to pick the tray up. Do waiters usually get help? How do you pick up a tray that heavy without spilling it?"

"Is that what you did? Spill it?"

"A little. But somehow I managed to pick up the tray and I headed for the door. Or the doors. They were those swinging doors. You know the ones I mean?"

"Like saloon doors?"

"Except made out of metal and bigger than the ones in cowboy movies."

"Yeah, I can picture them."

"Ever since that day, I've noticed that waiters with trays usually back out of those doors, using their butt and shoulders to open them. But I didn't think about it then. I shuffled forward instead of backward. I had to use my hands and tray to open the doors."

"And then you spilled the drinks?"

"Nope. I made it through the doors. Or I thought I had. Instead of swinging closed behind me, the doors must have swung back into the kitchen and then kept swinging the other way, because as I looked across the restaurant at my coworkers watching the game, as I imagined their reaction when I showed up with their drinks, the doors thudded into my back."

"And you spilled the drinks?"

"I spilled ALL of the drinks. The glasses crashed and shattered and the shards floated in the puddle of beer. Did I say puddle? I should have said pond. All the customers who had been watching the TVs were now looking at me."

"And that's when they banned you?"

"Nope. Employees came running from the kitchen and the rest of the restaurant to take care of the mess, but they didn't talk to me or even seem to notice me. It was like when an ambulance arrives and all the attention is focused on the patient."

"So . . . ?"

"So I walked back to my table—partly in a daze, partly mortified by what my co-workers would say."

"What did they say?"

"Nothing. They hadn't noticed what happened. Unlike the others in the restaurant, they hadn't stopped watching the game. I just sat down, sighing with relief. Have you ever almost gotten in a car accident—like, slid or even spun on the ice—but then driven away without a scrape? That's what this felt like."

"If you got away with it, why were you kicked out?"

"Because I went back."

"Into the kitchen?!"

"The guy next to me never took his eyes from the game but he said, 'Did you get those drinks?'"

"And you said, 'I talked with a waiter and they said they'll be here soon.'"

"I wish. I slid out of my chair and made another beeline."

"Another tray was there?"

"Sure was."

"And you picked it up again?"

"Sure did."

"And . . . no, you didn't. You did not spill the drinks again. You'd learned your lesson."

"I thought I had. I backed through the swinging doors this time instead of pushing them. I made sure they closed securely instead of kept swinging. I'd made it. I had a new lease on life. Or that's what I was thinking as I kept backing up. It's ironic, really. Had I been moving forward like the last time, I would have seen how there was still liquid on the floor. I would have seen how slippery it was. I would have spotted the yellow plastic sign that said

'Caution: Wet Floor.'"

"You slipped on the puddle YOU had made a few minutes earlier?"

"Glass everywhere. Beer everywhere."

"This time the staff noticed you."

"And my co-workers. Never lived it down. Pretty sure that's one of the reasons I've been stuck in Archives ever since, organizing the files. They don't trust someone who is a walking blooper reel to do real work."

"So . . . my house for the game, then?"

"Sounds good to me."

Paul

"I have to divorce Amy."

"Whoa."

"What she did is unforgivable."

"What did she do?"

"Are you ready for this?"

"Ready."

"Are you sitting down?"

"On my couch."

"Are you bracing yourself?"

"I think so? My arm is on the armrest. Does that count?"

"Are you strapped in?"

"Sorry, no. No seat belts in sight."

"How about some rope? Or a weighted blanket?"

"BRO."

"At least a fairly heavy blanket?"

"I'm hanging up."

"Last night she said she was too tired to watch TV."

"And then..."

"You don't understand. We've been bingeing the show every night."

"I actually thought you might be serious, bro."

"I am serious. You haven't heard the worst part."

"I'm listening."

"It was the season finale."

"Okay, that's pretty bad."

"Unforgivable. I hate my job—have I mentioned that?"

"A few trillion times."

"The one thing I have to look forward to all day is our show."

"And spending time with your wife and kid."

"This IS spending time with my wife."

"Does she know how you feel?"

"I gasped and gave her the silent treatment. She's aware of my dismay."

"And she's done nothing to repair the breach?"

"She said she'd be happy to watch if we got a TV in our bedroom. She likes being snuggled up in bed instead of going up and down the stairs at night."

"Nice. Problem solved."

"Problem not solved. I don't want a TV in our bedroom and she knows it."

"You don't?"

"No way."

"Why not?"

"Because we Americans are too addicted to TV. Not every room needs to have a TV in it."

"What's amazing is that this conversation makes total sense to you in your head, doesn't it?"

"Yep. In my mind, the logic is unimpeachable."

"You've got one screwed up mind."

"Yes, yes I do."

Paul

"Hey, man. You know what my main problem is with people who use the phrase 'family values'?"

"What?"

"They never talk about the most important values."

"Love and kindness and empa--"

"No. I mean, yes—those are important. And they don't talk about them. But they're not the most important."

"They aren't?"

"No. I mean, yes--they are the most important. But they're not the most universal."

"They aren't?"

"There are values that are based on pure logic and common sense that we should all agree on."

"Such as . . ."

"Don't clean the house before company comes over."

"You think that's a family value?"

"It should be. Cleaning the house before guests arrive is detrimental to our communities and our society as a whole."

"Do tell."

"We clean our house because we're afraid of being judged for being messy, right?"

"I guess so, yeah."

"That means we don't trust the people coming over to see how we actually live. Before they've even arrived, we've decided these people--our friends or family, usually--can't be trusted to not be judgy dickheads. I mean, we never even give them a chance to not be judgy dickheads. We just assume that's what they are. Following so far?"

"Picking up what you're laying down."

"So then these people come in, look at the house, and assume either 1) they live like shameful slobs by comparison, or 2) their friends think they're judgy dickheads. Either way, they now know the other people, the ones who own the cleaned house, are judgy dickheads themselves."

"That's a lot of judgy dickheads."

"So what do they do when they have people over?"

"The first judgy dickheads or the second?"

"The ones who were guests in the last scenario. What do they do when they become the hosts?"

"Clean their place?"

"Clean their place."

"Terrifying."

"Downfall of society. Our homes may be spotless, but the ties that bind us have been dragged in the mud until they fray. Everybody assumes everyone's a judgy dickhead, and all because we spent the day cleaning the house and then, when our guests arrived—this is the most insidious part—told them, 'Excuse the mess.'"

"So you're having people over, huh?"

"I'm not talking about me. I'm talking about universal family values."

"Amy wants you to help clean the house?"

"Another family value: do not, under any circumstances, write a thank you card. Why? Because they've become expected-- which renders them a chore for the writer and meaningless for the recipient."

"Are Heather and I invited?"

"We've robbed ourselves of the experience of giving and getting spontaneous, genuine gratitude."

"We'll bring noodle salad. The kind with the pepperoni. Store bought. And afterward, I expect you to send me a thank you card."

Paul

"I'm in trouble."

"How can I help, bro?"

"And it's all your fault."

"What is?"

"Did you or did you not tell Heather that you and I texted after the game?"

"I think so?"

"I know so."

"Ummmm. We *did* text after the game, dude."

"I know that. But thanks to Heather, Amy knows that too."

"Still not following."

"Amy knows I texted with you after the game . . . but didn't text with her."

"You didn't? Why not?"

"We'd just won the conference for the first time in two decades—and I was there! In attendance! I got to storm the field!"

"I know, man. You sent me the pictures. That's why we were texting."

"Right. But that's not why she was texting. She was texting me to ask when I'd be home."

"Seems reasonable."

"She wanted me to pick something up for dinner."

"Practical."

"This was no time to be practical. It was a bucket list experience. She was reminding me to bring the bucket home like it was Tupperware at a family get-together."

"And you told her all this?"

"Didn't get a chance. When I got home she asked me why I hadn't responded to the texts and I said my phone must not have had good reception."

"Which is when she said your phone seemed to have good enough reception for my texts."

"It was an ambush."

"Yikes."

"Betrayed by my best friend."

"You know, there's a lesson in here."

"Nothing is sacred?"

"If you're going to go to a conference championship, make sure you take your brother with you. That way, you won't need to text with him."

"I knew it! It was a set-up!"

"I plead the 5th."

"You were jealous of my bucket, so you kicked it when I wasn't looking."

"I PLEAD THE 5TH."

Agent E

"You need help."

"Ma'am?"

"Serious help."

"You're worried about my mental faculties, ma'am?"

"Well, yes, but—"

"I'm fine, ma'am."

"You're failing in your mission. He's not making any progress."

"I wouldn't say failing. Plateaued, perhaps."

"You're in denial."

"I don't think so, ma'am."

"See?"

"Yes, I see what you did there."

"You need help."

"A psychiatrist, ma'am?"

"A partner."

Paul

"Did you get her back to sleep, Paul?"

"Didn't have to. She was already out by the time I got there."

"I'm telling you, it's the new stuffed animal. She's been cuddling that bunny ever since she got it this morning. The doctor was right. She just needed the extra security."

"Speaking of: Why does it have Band-Aids all over it?"

"We put them on when we got home. To cover up all the places where stuffing was falling out."

"Its stuffing is falling out?"

"Its stuffing *was* falling out. It's not anymore."

"Because of the Band-Aids."

"Because of the Band-Aids."

"Maybe we should stitch it up?"

"Who's we? I'm no seamstress. By all means, go ahead."

"Band-Aids it is. Why'd you pick the one with stuffing coming out? Weren't there other stuffed animals on the shelf?"

"Dozens. But I didn't pick it. She did. Every time I tried to switch it out for another one, she screamed and hugged it tighter."

"Still is. Its snout is in the crook of her arm. Although . . . would you call that a hug? Looks more like she's suffocating it."

"It's crazy. One second we're quietly moving through the toy aisle. Then some blowhard behind me yells, 'Pump the breaks, lady!'"

"And they were talking to you?"

"I don't know. Probably not. Hopefully not. But I stopped instinctively and turned around. The voice sounded so close."

"And . . . ?"

"And there was no one there. But as I turned, our daughter lunged out of the cart and grabbed this bunny."

"Lunged?"

"Her butt was airborne. She hasn't let go of it since."

"Weird."

"Cute. True love."

"Love at first sight? That's your theory?"

"And I'm sticking to it."

"Works for me. Especially if it helps her sleep."

Agent E

"Did you pick up the Asset?"

"That's one way to put it, ma'am."

"Was there a problem?"

"A hitch, ma'am."

"Care to elaborate?"

"Permission to speak freely?"

"Granted."

"He won't shut up, ma'am."

"He's the best pilot we've got."

"And the loudest."

"What happened?"

"Permission to—"

"Granted, now and ten seconds from now, should you feel compelled to ask again."

"He yelled at my mother, ma'am."

"What do you mean?"

"Told her to, and I quote, 'pump the breaks' as she passed the drop-off spot."

"And she heard him?"

"I'd wager people in the parking lot heard him, ma'am."

"And she spotted him?"

"Negatory. She assumed a human source for the voice in question."

"No harm, no foul, then."

"My ear drums and my vocal cords beg to differ, ma'am."

"Agent?"

"As previously aforesaid, ma'am, he won't shut up."

"Had to drown out his screams with your own—that it?"

"That is indeed it, ma'am."

"Have you tried muzzling techniques?"

"To the point of suffocation, ma'am."

"Jesus. Is he all right? Is that the hitch? Do we have to tag and bag him on the first day?"

"Negatory, ma'am. The Asset's vitals remain intact."

"In that case, put him on the line. I'll talk to him."

"That won't be possible, ma'am. The Asset is . . . indisposed to talk."

"Oh my God. Did you remove his vocal cords?"

"No, ma'am."

"His tongue?"

"No, ma'am. He's indisposed merely for the nonce."

"The nonce?"

"The time being, ma'am."

"I still don't get it."

"Tranquilizer dart."

"Tranquilizer dart?"

"Tranquilizer dart, ma'am."

"Yikes. You don't play around, do you?"

"Desperate straits, ma'am."

"But this can't be a permanent solution."

"Understood, ma'am."

"He isn't the best pilot if he's not conscious."

"Undoubtedly not, ma'am."

"If there's nothing else . . . "

"Nothing for now, ma'am."

"He's the best pilot we've got, Agent."

"So you keep saying, ma'am."

Paul

"AHHHHHHHHHHHHHHHHHHHHHHHHHHHHHHHHHHHHHH!"

"Paul?!"

"They . . . They WON!"

"You woke me up, Paul."

"It's a miracle!"

"You woke the baby."

"4th down, no time left on the clock. How? HOW? I don't understand how they did it!"

"Whoa. It *is* a miracle."

"Right? Did you see that catch? That throw?"

"Not that. The baby. She stopped crying."

"Jump around and dance with me!"

"Gladly!"

Agent E & the Asset (at the same time as the previous page)
"NOOO—"

"WAHHHHHHHHHHHHHHHHHHHHHHHHHHHHHHHHHHHH
HHHH—"

"THEY LOST!"

"WAHHHHHHHHHHHHHHHHHHHHHHHHHHHHHHHHHHHH
HHHHHHH—"

"YOU CHUMPS!"

"WAHHHHHHHHHHHHHHHHHHHHHHHHHHHHHHHHHHHH
HHHHHHH—"

"YOU BUMS!"

"WAHHHHHHHHHHHHHHHHHHHHHHHHHHHHHHHHHHHH
HHHHHHH—"

"BUNCH OF BUSH LEAGUERS!"

"WAHHHHHHHHHHHHHHHHHHHHHHHHHHHHHHHHHHHH
HHHHHHH—"

"GRABBING DEFEAT FROM THE JAWS OF VICTORY!"

"WAHHHHHHHHHHHHHHHHHHHHHHHHHHHHHHHHHHHH
HHHHHHH—"

"Okay, sorry—got it out of my system.

"WAHHHHHHHHHHHHHHHHHHHHHHHHHHHHHHHHHHH HHHHHHH—"

"You can stop boo-hooing."

"WAHHHHHHHHHHHHHHHHHHHHHHHHHHHHHHHHHHH HHHHHHH—"

"I'll zip it, Agent, I swear."

"WAHHHHHHHHHHHHHHHHHHHHHHHHHHHHHHHHHHH HHHHHHH—"

"I'm putting away my screen."

"WAHHHHHHHHHHHHHHHHHHHHHHHHHHHHHHHHHHH HHHHHHH—"

"I'm whispering, okay? Is that better?"

"Quite."

Paul

"Amy."

"Paul."

"Our child is a top-notch negotiator."

"True."

"She can turn the tables like nobody's business."

"You're telling me things I already know."

"Remember all those books we read before she was born? The ones that said the trick was to give kids two options? That way, they think they're making a choice but really they're doing what you want them to do?"

"Yeah, that's never worked on her."

"Right? Never."

"Preaching to the choir."

"Tonight I asked her if she wanted to go to bed now or keep playing for five minutes and then go to bed. She looked at me like I was nuts. Like, *what kind of cockamamie outfit you runnin', old man?* Like, *neither, Dad. How'd you even come up with the crazy idea that I ever wanted to go to bed?*"

"Ha. So what did you do?"

"I didn't know what to do—so I just repeated myself. Except this time I kneeled down to her level. Actually, I stayed just a little above her, because I heard somewhere that talk show hosts do that as a power play. I looked right at her. I held her gaze. I didn't blink. I heard that somewhere too: if you don't blink, people will subconsciously pay more attention because they'll be waiting in suspense for your eyelids to shut. It's kind of like how Winston Churchill put a pin in his cigars so the ash got longer and longer, and people sat on the edge of their seats, waiting for it to fall."

"Is that true? About Winston Churchill?"

"It's true that someone told me that, yes."

"Ha."

"Anyway, I looked our three-year-old in the eye and instead of asking a question, I made two statements: You can go to bed now or in five minutes. I think she was impressed—I really do. We sat there silently for a few moments. I had my hand poised, ready to shake hers as soon as she made her decision."

"You were going to shake her hand?"

"I was going to seal the bedtime deal. I'd put my hand out, palm down, because that establishes dominance."

"It does?"

"According to a seminar at work it does."

"You spent time at work working on handshakes?"

"Moves and countermoves to establish hegemony, baby."

"Jesus. How awful."

"Agreed."

"How stupid."

"No argument from me."

"We've got to get you out of there."

"I don't want to get into that again. Where was I?"

"Establishing hegemony."

"Right."

"Did she counter your move?"

"You could say that."

"What, did she . . . twist your hand?"

"Nope."

"Ooooooh, I know! Did she sandwich your hand between both of her hands? That's gotta be a power move, right?"

"It is, but nope, she didn't do that."

"What did she do?"

"She reached out her hand . . . and picked my nose."

"What?!"

"I kid you not. Swiped her little fingernail right through my nostril."

"Ew. Did she . . . come up with anything?"

"She sure did. And then she wiped if off on the back of my hand."

"Ew again."

"More like awe. I'm in awe of her."

"Wait. Where is she? Is she not in bed? Paul, it was your turn to put her to bed and—"

"She's in bed."

"Really? How?"

"I have no idea. She picked her pajamas, brushed her teeth and chose a book for us to read—all without a word."

"In that case, good work. You did it."

"I honestly don't think I did a single thing."

Paul

"My daughter has an evil twin."

"You mean she has two different personalities?"

"No, I mean she—they—can be in two different places."

"Nice, bro."

"Last night we did the whole bedtime routine. I got her her snack, I waited for her to go potty, I helped her brush her teeth, I put on her lotion, I helped her put on her pajamas, I read to her, I rocked her in her rocking chair, I rubbed her back, I tucked her in exactly right with her feet out of the blanket, I kissed her forehead, I said goodnight."

"That's your routine? As in, you do it every night?"

"Every. Night."

"How long does all that take?"

"Between 45 minutes and forever."

"Sounds exhausting."

"You mean for me, but last night it seemed exhausting for her too. She yawned. Her eyelids looked heavy. She said, 'Night night, Daddy.'"

"Adorable."

"Triumphant. Mission: Bedtime was complete. I left her room and made my way down the hallway and into my bedroom, a job well done. I plopped onto my bed, turned onto my back, AND THERE SHE WAS."

"There who was?"

"My daughter. My other daughter. The evil twin. She must have been in my room the whole time."

"No chance she didn't just follow you out of her room?"

"Did you hear what I said? She YAWNED. Said goodnight."

"Night night."

"Exactly. You think she got out of bed and followed me down the hall without making a peep or creak? How fleet of foot do you think she is? How stealthy?"

"I mean, she IS Agent E."

"Still. Besides, the girl in my room had a runny nose. One might even say the sniffles."

"Didn't she just start daycare? I thought every kid gets sick in daycare."

"My daughter's nose was dry when I left her room."

"Maybe she—"

"Occam's razor, man."

"Occam's razor?"

"The simplest explanation is the right one."

"You think an evil twin is the simplest explanation?"

"You got any other ideas?"

"You were at your child's birth; doesn't Occam think you would have noticed another kid?"

"Amy had a c-section."

"You're saying one slipped out below while the other came out above?"

"I'm saying there was a curtain blocking Amy's and my view. We couldn't see what was going on on the other side."

"You're right. It's settled. Evil twin is the only solution."

"They can't fool me."

"Unless . . . A clone, perhaps? Another kid wearing a mask that looks just like your daughter's face? CGI in real life? If you think about it, the possibilities are endless."

"Now you're being ridiculous."

"You're right. I'm sorry."

Agent E

"A bit of an audible with your body double, Agent."

"Yes, ma'am."

"The double is supposed to go to daycare for you, so you can concentrate on your mission."

"Yes, ma'am."

"Was there a reason you concocted this little sleight of hand?"

"Parenting doesn't begin and end at the threshold of my room, ma'am."

"And your father doesn't know that?"

"He'll yawn while reading me to sleep, then have a skip in his step as he leaves, ma'am."

"Which hurts your feelings?"

"No, which shows me he has reserves stored up elsewhere that he refuses to tap into until after he thinks the parenting is done. The parenting is never done, ma'am."

"Don't we all do that? Don't we all need a break from something?"

"I suppose so, ma'am. But we don't make it so obvious."

"And that hurts your feelings."

"This isn't about feelings, ma'am. I wouldn't expend all these resources for something as trivial as feelings."

"Isn't that why we expend most of our resources?"

Paul

"I'm just saying, Paul—wouldn't you rather change your job than complain about it?"

"Everyone complains about their job, Amy. You were complaining about yours the other day."

"I was complaining about donuts. Someone brought donuts for the office and all that was left were crumbs by the time I got back from my meeting."

"Exactly. If it's not one thing it's another."

"I didn't pump my arms as I ran for the liquor cabinet when I got home, Paul."

"You would have if your job was bursting people's pipe dreams."

"The point is that my job isn't bursting people's pipe dreams. And yours doesn't have to be either."

"Applying for another job is a job in and of itself."

"Okay, Paul."

"In this economy, I'm lucky to have the job I already have."

"You have the hiccups, Paul."

"Scare me. That's the best way to stop hiccups."

"The fact that it's 5:00 in the afternoon and you have drunk hiccups should be all the scaring you need."

Agent E

With one hand, Agent E muzzles the Asset's nose, mouth.

For God's sake, she thinks, *aren't bunnies known for their silence?*

Still, she can't help using her other hand to muffle a snicker of her own.

"You want to be scared, Old Boots?" she thinks to herself. "The game is afoot...."

Paul

"How's Agent E doing, bro o' mine?"

"She may not be a good super spy after all."

"No?"

"No. We were training yesterday and—"

"Hold up—you were training?"

"Playing Hide and Seek."

"Ah."

"What could be better practice for a life of stealth and cunning?"

"And your trainee didn't perform up to standards?"

"It was pretty dismal. I'd cover my eyes, tell her to hide. Then I'd say, 'Ready or not, here I come!' and uncover my eyes."

"Standard operating procedure."

"Exactly. I followed protocol to a T."

"But the kid wouldn't be ready?"

"Nope."

"No hiding at all?"

"Worse. She did try to hide. In the exact same place as the last time."

"You sound disappointed."

"I *was* disappointed. Each time I'd close my eyes and think, 'Okay, this time she'll find a different place. She'll crawl out from behind the couch and hide behind the chair instead, or under the table, or anywhere else. I even went around the room, pretending to look in those places, trying to give her some new ideas. But the whole charade was pointless. The whole time I'd see her from the corner of my eye, still behind the damn couch."

"Wait. You could see her?"

"That was the worst part. Not only was she in the same spot, but she had situated herself in such a way that I could still see her or Band-Aid Bunny wherever else I looked."

"Band-Aid Bunny?"

"Her stuffed animal."

"Gotcha."

"I thought she'd graduated past the covering her own eyes and thinking she'd vanished from view—but it appeared she'd regressed. There she was, sitting basically out in the open, over and over, and she wasn't even covering her eyes."

"But you pretended you couldn't see her?"

"What else was I going to do? I didn't want to hurt her feelings."

"What a guy."

"Are you there? Or there? How about there? Oh where oh where could you be? I felt like a chump."

"How did you decide when to find her?"

"When I couldn't stand it any longer. When my respect for myself and for her overcame me. I'd be like, 'Wait a second, I know she can't possibly be behind this couch.' Then I'd reach behind the couch and "accidentally" tap her head or grab Band-Aid Bunny by the paw and, 'Eureka! THERE you are!'"

"Really milking it."

"Exactly. I needed to do something to amuse myself. Besides, I told myself, it wasn't her fault she had no stealth. I was trying to come up with future careers where inability to blend in was a good thing. Maybe she could be an air traffic controller on a tarmac when she grows up."

"Ha."

"That's what I was thinking as I reached yet again for Band-Aid Bunny. I pulled at his paw . . . but there was no resistance."

"No resistance?"

"No opposing force holding onto the other paw. The stuffed animal lifted right up. I craned my neck, peered further over the couch. And the kid wasn't there."

"She wasn't?"

"Nope. She'd disappeared."

"Whoa."

"That's when she tapped me."

"She was behind you?"

"Honestly, she might as well have jolted me with an electric prod. That's how shocked I was."

"You sound so proud, dude."

"All this time I thought her future as a super spy was dashed . . . but she was setting me up. She was lulling me into a false sense of security, and luring me in with her stuffed animal."

"Impressive."

"And I didn't tell you the best part. I had some post-drunk hiccups. And this little sneak attack wiped them right out."

"Why were you getting drunk on a Tuesday?"

"Can we focus on my daughter the secret agent?"

"I thought you said at the beginning of this conversation that she wasn't a good super spy."

"She's not. She's a GREAT super spy."

"I see. It was a set-up."

"I learned from the best."

Paul

"Paul. What are you watching?"

"*A Few Good Men.*"

"The Tom Cruise one? You can't handle the truth?"

"Yeah."

"I thought you owned it."

"I do."

"Then why are you watching it on network TV?"

"I like the commercials."

"Are you feeling okay, Paul?"

"Huh? I'm fine."

"You LIKE the commercials? No one likes the commercials."

"They're nostalgic."

"You miss the days when you needed to sit through commercials?"

"Sort of. Reminds me of high school, when I first saw *A Few Good Men.*"

"The first time you saw A Few Good Men was on TV?"

"Hmmmm? Oh. Maybe. We might have rented it; I don't remember. But I first saw it back when watching TV always included commercials."

"And you miss that?"

"I miss thinking I would be Tom Cruise."

"You wanted to be an actor?"

"A lawyer."

"You did?"

"I used to sign my name in yearbooks 'Paul Hoblin, Attorney At Law'."

"So what happened?"

"Why are you smirking?"

"I'm not. I'm smiling."

"About what?"

"You signing yearbooks like that."

"You think it's dorky?"

"No. I mean yes. Of course. You're a total dork. But I like the idea of you thundering around a courtroom."

"Think I could do it?"

"You already thunder around social media."

"Courtroom of public opinion."

"So what happened?"

"What do you mean?"

"Why didn't you become Tom Cruise?"

"I would have had to go to law school."

"You didn't realize that?"

"Just seemed like a lot of work."

"You didn't fulfill your yearbook dream because it would have been a lot of work?"

"I'd answer that, but the commercial break is ending."

Agent E

Tonight, like every night this week, Agent E finds herself glad that babies don't sweat.

Hyperbole, of course.

Their skin—her skin—dampens.

But it doesn't drip.

And thank God for that.

As she descends from the heavens (or, more accurately, the ceiling fan), she shudders at the thought of a single droplet releasing from the tip of her nose and splashing like a bucket of water across one of her parents' erstwhile sleeping faces.

She hears the Asset grunt.

"Mea culpa," she thinks, knowing it was her shudder that caused his grunt.

She pictures the Asset in her mind's eye: above her, lowering the rope attached to her back, grimacing with exertion, braced on a fan blade.

"Ironic," she thinks. All this effort so the Asset can spend the rest of the night speaking as loudly as he'd like without blowing their cover—but what if it's this very effort that gives them away?

It's not. Not tonight, anyway.

Agent E, hovering mere centimeters from her parents' twitching, REM-cycled eyelids, makes quick work of installing the plugs in each of their four ears.

A hand gesture later and the Asset is hauling her up again.

She breathes a silent sigh of relief. They'll have to do the whole thing again in a few hours, of course. What was installed must be uninstalled. But for the time being, the tense and ticklish work is over.

The gust of her parents' snores only aid in her ascent.

"SAYONARA, SUCKERS!" the Asset says once she has alighted on the next blade. "LET'S BLOW THIS POPSICLE STAND TO SLIVERS!"

Paul

"My kid is waging germ warfare against me, man."

"Sounds about right."

"Sounds dastardly, is what it sounds. I swear, she got herself sick just so she could infect her target."

"Which would be you."

"I'm walking through my living room when she yells, 'Catch!' Out of the corner of my eye I see her standing on the arm of the couch. Before I know what's happening, she crouches down and launches herself at me."

"And did you?"

"Did I what?"

"Catch her? Like she told you to do?"

"I fell right into her trap. She landed into my arms with a jolt. Knocked the wind out of me. I gasped. And as I was gasping, she was coughing . . . right into my open mouth."

"Bullseye."

"Target eliminated."

"Sorry your kid's under the weather, man."

"I can feel the mucus building in the back of my throat."

"And I thought kids didn't like to share."

"If I survive this attack, I'm wearing a gas mask from here on out."

Paul

"Why do you think your parents gave you a snack every night before bedtime?"

"What?"

"No judgment, I swear. Did you not eat enough for dinner?"

"No. I mean yes. I mean—"

"It just seems like, in our case, there's no real upside. She eats less for dinner because she knows she'll get a snack. She's more likely to pee in her pull-up at night because of all the water and milk we give her minutes before tucking her in. I'm just wondering why your parents thought it was worth it to ply you with food and drink every night?"

"Wait. Are you trying to—"

"Criticize? No! I swear! The snack is what it is. You're a great mom. Your mom and dad are great too. I've just never understood the purpose of the bedtime snack. Is it tradition? Did one or both of their parents do the same thing?"

"Your parents didn't give you a bedtime snack?"

"No. But I'm not comparing! It's totally fine that your parents did. Just wondering why they—"

"Paul, my parents didn't give me a bedtime snack."

"Yes they did."

"No, they didn't."

"They didn't? Then why do we give our daughter one?"

"I've been wondering the same thing for two years. I assumed it's what you had grown up with."

"What I grew up with?"

"Your parents didn't give you a snack every night?"

"If your parents didn't give you a bedtime snack, then why did you start giving our daughter one?"

"I thought you started it."

"No way."

"Two years."

"Two. Years."

Paul

"Amy doesn't take me seriously."

"This is something that matters to you? You have a need to be taken seriously?"

"When I'm being serious I do. When I have serious stuff to talk about."

"Fair enough, bro. *I'll* take you seriously. What serious stuff were you trying to say to Amy?"

"I don't remember. That's not the point."

"It isn't?"

"No, it isn't. It doesn't matter what the serious stuff is—what matters is that it was serious, and Amy laughed right in my face."

"Maybe she wasn't laughing at you."

"If you say maybe she was laughing with me, I'm hanging up."

"No, man—I'm saying maybe she wasn't laughing *at* you. Like, you're assuming she was laughing at your words. But maybe her laughing had nothing to do with what you were saying."

"It just happened to sync up perfectly to me approaching her and starting to speak?"

"Exactly."

"Just pure coincidence? Some random fleeting funny thought flit into her head at the exact moment I opened my mouth to speak? That's your theory?"

"It doesn't have to be totally random. Was your fly down?"

"What? No."

"Does your shirt have pit stains? Did you have something in your teeth?"

"These aren't even things Amy finds funn . . . "

"Dude? You there?"

"Dammit."

"What?"

"You're right."

"I am?"

"She wasn't laughing right in my face. She was laughing right at my face."

"I knew it. Something in your teeth?"

"Chalk."

"In your teeth?"

"On my face. All over my face."

"Because . . .?"

"Makeup. Makeover. Earlier today the kid dipped the chalk in a puddle and pretended it was lipstick, eye shadow, blush for my face."

"This was her idea?"

"Unclear. It all happened rather quickly. I definitely went along with it."

"I thought you liked being taken seriously."

"She *was* taking me seriously. Or least she was taking her task seriously. She was dead-set on making me the belle of the ball. I admired her focus."

"Is that why you didn't wash it off?"

"I didn't wash it off because I didn't remember it was there."

"Who could blame you? You had important stuff that you also don't remember to tell your wife."

"I marched up to her with colorful crud all over my face. She must've been watching it flake off as I spoke."

"Glad we got this cleared up."

"I'm looking in a mirror now. My face looks like it's covered in dried-out, crusty unicorn vomit."

Agent E

"Is that what you were trying to do, Agent? Help your father learn not to take himself so seriously?"

"Let's go with that, ma'am."

"Why else would you smear his face in chalk?"

"A true artist can paint on any canvas, ma'am."

"Wait. Is he right? Were *you* taking yourself seriously?"

"It looked nothing like unicorn vomit, ma'am."

"No need to get defensive, Agent."

"I'm not being defensive, ma'am. *He* was being *offensive*. Anyone who could fail to appreciate the way my shading accentuated his cheekbones is either a lout or a liar."

"It was your mother who laughed."

"So says the lout."

Paul

"It's basically official at this point, Amy."

"What is?"

"Teachers are the enemy."

"It's really sad."

"Teachers, Amy."

"I know."

"The ones setting up book mobiles, greeting students at classroom doors, staying so late grading papers after school that their classroom light turns off and they have to wave their arms to sensor them back on."

"How do you know they do that?"

"It's what I have to do when I stay late at the office—why would it be any different for them?"

"Do most schools even have sensors for their lights?"

"Good point. It's probably not in the budget."

"The whole thing just makes me sad."

"It makes me angry. I mean, are you kidding me? Teachers? The ones sporting Great Clips haircuts and whiteboard marker-smudged hands? The ones counting student heads on buses before and after field trips? The ones with rings on their desks from coffee mugs and rings under their eyes from getting up early and staying late?"

"You already wrote that line on Facebook, didn't you?"

"No. Yes. So?"

"Nothing. It's a good line."

"Teachers, Amy. Public enemy #1. They must be watched. Monitored. Bugged. Clandestinely caught. Publicly pilloried."

"You're blatantly reading from your post now. The alliteration is a dead giveaway."

"You, over there, when you're finished with your lunch duty, turn yourself in to the proper authorities for interrogation."

"Really, really scary."

"History teachers have already gotten fired for teaching . . . wait for it . . . history. Doing their job is now against the law."

"Are you going to do anything about it besides read to me?"

"I was thinking of becoming a lawbreaker myself."

"Really?"

"I mean a teacher. That was my dramatic way of saying maybe I could become a teacher."

"I caught that."

"Now is when you're supposed to look concerned."

"It is?"

"Teachers somewhat famously don't make much money, Amy."

"Yes, I heard that somewhere."

"They're underappreciated."

"Clearly."

"Given all these new laws, I might not have any job security."

"True."

"And from what I've read, they're currently leaving the profession in droves."

"I saw that too."

"Why aren't you trying to talk me out of this?"

"Why did you think I would?"

"Wishful thinking, I suppose."

Paul

"She walked into the bathroom while I was peeing. Stood there, watching me. Then she said, 'Daddy? Why is your tail in front?'"

"Your tail?"

"It's not funny, Amy."

"What did you tell her?"

"Nothing. She made her announcement and left."

"So now, in her world, boys have tails."

"In front."

"Will she think all animals with tails are boys?"

"Will she think animals pee out of their tails?"

"We should figure out what we want to say to her."

"Agreed."

"The key is to have a unified front."

"Please, no more talk of fronts."

Agent E

"I didn't know what else to say, ma'am."

"A tail?"

"Sauntered in to splash water on my face and there he was. There *it* was."

"So you called it a tail?"

"My mind was racing, ma'am. I was trying to think of something, anything, from my frame of reference."

"And what you came up with was a tail."

"I dare say your amusement is excessive, ma'am."

"It was better than saying nothing, I suppose. Just staring and then leaving. That would have traumatized him even more. He would have spent the rest of his life walking around with his tail between his legs."

"Hardy har har, ma'am."

Paul

"Hey, bro."

"What were you thinking?"

"What was I thinking . . . "

"When you got us the inflatable dragon sledding tube?"

"I did? I did. We did. For Agent E's birthday."

"I repeat: what were you thinking?"

"We weren't."

"No, you weren't."

"I mean, I'm pretty sure we got it off a registry Amy made. It wasn't our idea."

"In that case, what was she thinking?"

"'Inflatable dragon sledding tube—looks fun!'?"

"Maybe it would be, if inflatable dragon sledding tubes were actually inflatable."

"Have you tried—"

"Blowing it up? Turns out a giant inflatable dragon takes more air than my lungs can produce. I could feel the dragon leeching oxygen from my brain. Pretty sure I passed out a couple times."

"You could—"

"Get a pump? Went to the store and got one. Brought it back. None of the nozzles fit the valve. Went back and got another one."

"Problem solved?"

"If inflatable dragon sledding tubes were meant for inside use, then sure. But apparently sledding takes place outside."

"And . . ."

"Inflatable dragon sledding tubes inflated with warm air deflate when faced with cold air."

"Do you have—"

"An outdoor outlet? Yep. Tucked behind a scratchy bush and a mound of snow. After shoveling away the mound and scratching my cheek against the bush, I got the pump plugged in. My hands are frostbitten because I had to take off my gloves to plug in the valve, but the inflatable dragon is now officially inflated."

"You're good to go!"

"I am, but my daughter isn't. While my fingers are turning black, she refuses to put on her mittens. Or her hat. Or her jacket."

"Because..."

"She'd just taken all those things off. She'd been standing by the door, all suited up, waiting for me to inflate the damn dragon. By the time I did, she was sweating and shedding. She's now boycotting all winter wear."

"Couldn't you—"

"Warm up the car, carry her to the car seat, and change her into her jacket when we get there? No, because the coldest place on earth is standing outside a warm car on a cold day, negotiating with a kid in a car seat. It's like Hoth from Star Wars, and the car is the tauntaun Han Solo slices open to keep Luke warm. Except in Star Wars Luke doesn't squirm around while Han tries to keep him warm and alive."

"Maybe you can try again next weekend."

"Oh, we're going today. This is supposed to be a fun sledding trip, dammit. Wonderful father-daughter bonding time. I don't care how miserable we are."

"Then why are we talking on the phone? Go have your miserable fun time."

"I can't figure out how to fit the inflatable dragon in the car."

Paul

"It finally happened, man."

"What?"

"Call Guinness."

"They're giving away free beer?"

"Guinness Book of World Records."

"You set a world record?"

"I had a conversation online with a random person and the conversation was truly productive."

"Whoa."

"Like, someone's mind was actually changed."

"About what?"

"I wrote one of my long posts about politics and the state of the world, and someone accused me of hypocrisy."

"Because . . ."

"Because the day before I'd written a post about my daughter putting a pea in her bellybutton."

"Did she really do that?"

"Sure did. I have photographic evidence to prove it, which I provided with my post."

"Why does your kid being a weirdo make you a hypocrite?"

"Because if I took the time to post a cute picture of my daughter, I'm clearly not as worried about our democracy as I claim to be. If I really thought we were on the brink of losing our democracy, I would be so consumed by this horrifying possibility that I wouldn't have the time or the inclination to post wacky family pictures."

"That's what you think?"

"It's what the random guy online thinks."

"And you think he has a point?"

"No. I think that's the dumbest point anyone has ever made."

"Okay..."

"It's shockingly stupid. Someone who faces a scary reality is obligated to face that reality 24/7? No laughter allowed? For a person to be taken seriously, they must forgo all other experiences and emotions? It's sociopathic. But mostly it's really, really stupid. If anything, it's the people who face up to harsh reality who most need to take a breather, to live their lives, to recharge."

"You told him all that?"

"Sure did. Called him a numb nuts. Then apologized for my language and said I should have just said numbskull."

"And he accepted your apology? He saw the error of his ways?"

"Ha. Yeah right."

"I thought minds were changed."

"They were. Well, mine was."

"He changed your mind?"

"Sort of. I realized, as I was deciding which part of his body was insensate, that, in my own novocaine brain, I had been making his exact argument."

"You had?"

"Yep. I'd been going back and forth between reading the news and reading the lack of news on my social media feeds and, man, I was in despair. Why is nobody talking about this threat to human existence? Why is nobody standing up for our world? Our country? Our communities? But talking with this guy gave me an epiphany."

"Impressive."

"Like, Eureka! People do care. They are aware. They are engaged. They're not sticking their heads in the sand."

"They're not?"

"Nope. They're just doing some self-care. Taking a breather. Coming up for air isn't the same thing as going down for sand."

"True...."

"What?"

"It's just.... Maybe you're right. Maybe people are secretly paying attention. But maybe..."

"Not? Maybe not? Is that what you were going to say?"

"It's a toss-up at best, right?"

"This is not helping with my despair."

"Sorry."

"From now on I'm going to stick with online trolls. Way more productive than talking with people I care about."

Agent E

"You stuck a pea in your bellybutton?"

"Seemed like the prudent thing to do, ma'am?"

"Prudent? A pea—in your bellybutton?"

"It's where the camera was, ma'am."

"So? Wasn't it concealed? I thought the navel-rendering was spot-on."

"The verisimilitude is indeed beyond reproach."

"So . . ."

"The camera had been jarred loose, ma'am."

"By . . ."

"By raspberry kisses, ma'am."

"I see. So you placed the pea to avoid detection."

"In the nick of time, ma'am."

"Still, we might want to move the camera back to its original position, Agent. More obstructed viewing, of course, but better safe than sorry."

"I've already relocated it to my nostril, ma'am."

"Good. That way, if comes loose again, you can—"

"Insert food or other objects accordingly."

"Our agents have been shoving stuff up their noses for as long as I can remember. Caretakers have somehow learned to expect it as normal."

"Understood, ma'am."

"Agent?"

"Ma'am?"

"Was it your mother who issued the raspberry kisses?"

"Negatory. Old Boots, ma'am."

"He's not an unloving father, Agent."

"Never said he was, ma'am."

"I'm just saying that love isn't the problem, Agent."

"No, but that doesn't mean he doesn't have a problem."

"Of course not. You're right. Proceed with the mission, Agent."

"I shall carry on, ma'am."

Paul

"The wife and kid are gone for the weekend."

"Yeah?"

"Girls trip with Amy's mom, sisters and their kids."

"Nice. That's nice, right?"

"Definitely. Finally have some time for myself."

"Totally, bro. Watch some adult TV. Drink some adult beverages. Should we get a poker game going?"

"Not sure I can squeeze it in."

"Already got big plans?"

"Oh yeah."

"What's on the docket?"

"Playing with my kid's stuff, mostly."

"You're serious, aren't you?"

"I'm building a giant tower out of blocks as we speak. And for the first time ever, the kid won't be here to knock it down before I finish."

"This will take you the whole weekend?"

"I also have Play-Doh to play with—all the canisters, not just the scraps she gives me. And coloring books to color without her suddenly flipping the page. And magnets that, according to the box, can be fashioned into complicated geometric structures."

"We could play poker at night. No kid to read to at bedtime means—"

"I CAN RAID HER BOOKSHELVES!"

"This is exciting to you?"

"She won't let me read certain books because she says only Mom's allowed to read them. But what's to stop me from reading *Uni the Unicorn* now? Hmmmmmm? Bwahahahahaha!"

"I'd ask if you're going to have a party at your place, but I'm afraid the answer is yes. And the party will include cake and Pin the Tail on the Donkey."

"No party. I'm going to clean my dishes and only my dishes. Then I'm going to bed at 8:30 for ten uninterrupted hours of shut-eye."

Paul

"Have you thought any more about teaching?"

"Too impractical."

"Law school?"

"I don't think it's for me, Ames."

"How come?"

"For one thing, I'm pretty sure I'd have to take a test."

"In law school? I'm sure you'd have to take many tests, Paul."

"I mean just to get in."

"You're not going to go to law school because you don't want to take a test?"

"It's more than that. I just don't think I'm interested in the law."

"What? I thought you *were* interested in becoming a lawyer. Did I miss something? Did I make up whole conversations in my head?"

"I'm interested in studying Constitutional law, but that's pretty much it. Property law, zoning laws, people getting in accidents, environmental law. I don't really know what all there is to study—but most of it sounds sort of boring to me."

"Okay . . . but Constitutional law is a thing, right?"

"Yeah."

"And you *are* interested in it?"

"I'm interested in, like, the big ideas. You know? Equality, fairness, becoming a more perfect union. I'm interested in what the Constitution actually says, but also what it means—what it has meant, what it can mean now and in the future. I keep trying to figure out what Constitutional scholars think about a pissant politician or some jackass on TV—and sometimes I find myself wishing I *was* that Constitutional scholar."

"So what's the problem?"

"The other stuff is important. The red tape. The local statutes. The legal loopholes. It's like politicians. We don't need more egomaniac senators; we need people on the city council and the school board."

"Okay..."

"I think deep down I just want to go toe to toe with the blowhards and have a leg to stand on."

"And that's a bad thing?"

"It's not a good thing."

"So let me get this straight: you not only know you are interested in going into law, you know what kind of law interests you. And when I say interests you, I mean obsesses you."

"I wouldn't go that far."

"I would. By the way, could you please start dimming your screen at night? Middle of the night and it's like you flipped on the light switch, all so you can look up one more expert opinion to put in another Facebook post."

"Sorry. I try to turn the phone away from you. I even lean over the bed so my phone is by the floor."

"See? Obsessed."

"And you want me to go to law school? What if that makes my obsession worse?"

"I want you to work as hard talking yourself into going to law school as you do talking yourself out of it."

"Being a lawyer won't make a better person."

"What if it makes you a happier person?"

Agent E

"DITCH THE DEAD WEIGHT."

"That's not an option, Asset."

"NOTHING MORE DANGEROUS THAN A DROWNING DUMBASS."

"My mission is to rescue said dumbass, no matter how much he flips out or flails."

"GO DOWN WITH THE SHIP?"

"Save the ship. Or salvage the parts. Look, I'm not bailing water for the boat's sake. I'm doing it for mine. I'm doing it for ours. All of ours. We've got agents with buckets all over the world. These vessels are taking on too much water—if we want to get anywhere, we have to take matters into our own hands."

"A SHIP THAT AIN'T SEAWORTHY IS A CASKET."

Paul

"Paul. PAUL!"

"Amy."

"You did it again."

"Left your phone perched on top of the toilet paper roll."

"Oh. Whoops."

"Stop doing that, Paul."

"I didn't mean to forget it, Amy. That's the whole point of forgetting. It's an accident."

"Stop putting your phone on the toilet paper. It's gross."

"Why is it gross? It's perched against the wall and the roll. If the paper's on the roll, it's still clean. That's why it's still part of the roll. When you unroll it, you're getting more clean toilet paper."

"I know how toilet paper works. I'm saying your phone is germy. You spend all day putting your germy fingers on it. The same germy fingers you just used to wipe."

"I think you're just jealous."

"I'm jealous."

"Yep. I came up with an ingenious way to treat going to the bathroom like going to the movies or a live sporting event. I'm telling you, the acoustics are great in here. You know how singing voices never sound better than when in the shower? Same concept. Sometimes I sit even when I'm peeing so I can get the full theater effect."

"One of these days your phone is going to fall into the toilet. And you won't get any sympathy from me."

"How is it going to fall into the toilet?"

"What do you mean how is it going to fall into the toilet? It's perched precariously on the toilet paper roll—and toilet paper rolls *roll*."

"No chance."

"No chance?"

"Nope. It's basic physics. The weight of the phone keeps the roll from rolling."

"What if I unroll the roll with the phone still on it?"

"Is that a threat?"

"No, I mean unwittingly. On automatic pilot. Sometimes I don't even look when I unroll toilet paper."

"Be that as it may."

"Be that as it may? What's that supposed to mean?"

"For one thing, I find it highly unlikely that you no-look your unrolling."

"Why?"

"Because you have to measure the squares before ripping. Everyone does. And even if you for some strange reason opt to unroll without eyeballing the roll, it still wouldn't fall into the toilet."

"Because . . ."

"Because you'd be sitting right there, in between the tumbling phone and the basin."

"There'd still be an opening."

"A crevice, at most. The odds of the phone splooshing are insurmountable. This isn't *Star Wars*. It isn't Luke Skywalker destroying the Death Star. This is real life."

"I'm honestly not sure it is. What are we even talking about?"

"Come to think of it, I think I'll watch *Star Wars* next time I'm in there."

Agent E

"11 games in a row, Agent?"

"I had a lesson in mind, ma'am."

"Which was . . ."

"Old Boots explained, after beating me in a game of *CandyLand*, that I shouldn't take it personally—that, indeed, he'd always possessed a flair for the fortuitous."

"A flair for the fortuitous? That's what he said?"

"He called it luck, ma'am. He said when it came to board games, Lady Luck had always been on his side."

"Not today, it sounds like."

"Not ever, ma'am."

"You're saying he's never lucky?"

"I'm saying one should never rely on nor take pride in luck. The way he was yammering, you'd think he'd done something to earn his victory."

"That's why you beat him eleven times in a row? To shut him up?"

"To remind him that sometimes—too often--there's no rhyme or reason. Our fortunes rise or fall depending on the mercurial whims of temperamental Chance. Fate is at once mirage and chimera; skill is often but a deft delusion. Just as the weatherman shall never truly master meteorology, so too shall humanity never direct its destiny. After all, if cause and effect were truly in our grasp, if some invisible force were truly putting its thumb on the scales for one's benefit, how to explain the age-old dilemma of innocent suffering?"

"And, in this analogy, you were the innocent doing the suffering?"

"Temporarily, ma'am."

"You can say that again. 11 games in a row? Now who's the lucky one?"

"The tables did indeed turn, ma'am."

"So you concede luck exists?"

"Oh, most definitely. I was lucky to be wearing my X-ray contact lenses. They allowed me to find the best cards from the pile."

"Ah-ha! So there was an invisible force playing favorites!"

"The game was, as they say, rigged."

"Did he learn his lesson?"

"Manifestly not, I'm afraid. He acted neither chastened nor deterred."

"How'd he act?"

"More prideful than ever, ma'am."

"After that shellacking? What in the world does he have to be proud of?"

"In a word, me."

"Oh! Fatherly love! That's sweet, no?"

"No. He seems to believe that, through genetic or cosmic transference, he has somehow passed on his luck to me. Improbably, this little episode affirmed his faith that Lady Luck remained by his side. Indeed, he's been calling me Fortuna all afternoon and has plans to take me on his next Vegas trip."

"Do you think Fortuna had X-ray contact lenses too?"

Paul

"I cut banana stickers."

"What?"

"Amy said today that I don't pay attention to or thank her for all she does for our family."

"Ouch. Did you apologize?"

"I said I was sorry she felt that way."

"May Day, bro. MAY DAY."

"I know."

"Judges say . . . not a true apology."

"Amy agreed with their ruling."

"Do you agree with them?"

"Yeah. But it was better than what I wanted to say."

"What did you want to say?"

"That she doesn't pay attention to or thank me for what I do for the family, either."

"You're right. That would have been worse."

"I cut the banana stickers."

"Still don't get it."

"The stickers. On the bananas. I cut them."

"Those round stickers on each banana peel? Why would you cut them?"

"No, not those. The big sticker. The long sticker. The one that wraps around the bushel and keeps it pressed together. Are several bananas called a bushel? A bunch? A . . ."

"No idea."

"Whatever it's called, it has a sticker wrapped around all the bananas. And I cut it."

"Okay."

"Snip it with a scissors."

"Well done?"

"You're damn right well done. If I didn't do it, no one would. Amy just tries to stretch the sticker enough to pry a banana from the bushel."

"No good?"

"A total pain. But I take matters and scissors into my own hands, for the sake of everyone who wants a banana."

"Your generosity knows no bounds."

"No fuss. No fanfare. No expectation of thanks from a grateful nation."

"A true team player, bro. Nay, a patriot."

"Citizenship requires a commitment to the common good. That's all I'm saying."

"Are we still talking about you and Amy?"

"She might keep track of our bills. And do our taxes. And do most of the laundry. And lots of other things."

"But you cut the banana stickers."

"Among other things."

"Such as?"

"I'm not into keeping tallies."

"Ah."

"I like to keep my heroism unsung."

"By singing your own praises?"

Paul

"Long time no talk, bro."

"I flatten boxes."

"What?"

"For the recycling. Amy just piles them on top of each other, but I flatten them so we can fit more into the recycling container."

"Did you just call me right back to tell me you flatten boxes?"

"I called you back to tell you yet another example of me contributing to the team without any need for validation or acknowledgment."

"Yes, clearly you don't need that."

"I'll let you know if I think of other feats of derring-do."

"Godspeed, man."

Paul

"Paul. Paul. PAUL."

"Hmmmm?"

"Are you up?"

"What's going on?"

"We need to move, Paul."

"Can we do it in the morning?"

"Bring only what you can carry. I'll get the car started."

"Does that include the kid?"

"Of course."

"She's getting pretty unwieldy."

"That's not funny, Paul."

"Why are you talking like you stole government secrets and the might of the government is descending upon us?"

"Mice, Paul."

"Mice, Amy?"

"They're in the walls. I can hear them scurrying. It creeps me out."

"I'll text our landlord tomorrow."

"Tomorrow?"

"It's the middle of the night, Amy. We can lay traps tomorrow, too."

"Why wait? Why not put them in our daughter's crib and snap off her fingers right now?"

"So no traps then. You have a better idea?"

"I told you. Flee."

"What, pray tell, are you doing?"

"PLAYING WHAC-A-MOUSE."

"Your plan is to lure said rodents out of the wall in order pistol whip them?"

"PISTOLS AREN'T FOR WHIPPING."

"Ah. Riddle the wall with bullets? Is that it?"

"FORGET CHEESE. EAT LED, MICE."

"Might I make a suggestion?"

"SHOOT."

"No. Quite the opposite. Don't shoot. For one thing, have you ever seen an action movie? It is impossible to shoot someone when they're on the roof of a subway train."

"THIS AIN'T NO SUBWAY TRAIN, SISTER."

"The principle holds, no? Perforating a barrier with bullets does not, however inexplicable, result in a pierced body on the other side."

"AIN'T NO MOVIE, EITHER."

"Fair enough. Are you not worried about blowing our cover as you blow away these rodents?"

"EAR PLUGS INTACT. MOM AND DAD INCAPACITATED."

"And the other residents of this apartment building?"

"SILENCER IN GUN. NIGHTY NIGHT EVERYONE."

"Well, it appears you've thought of everything, except—"

"REST IN WAR, CRITTERS!"

"—for the giant holes all over the walls."

"DAMN."

"Slipped your mind?"

"DAMNATION, POPULATION ME."

"No exit strategy, Agent?"

"THESE GUNS ARE MY EXIT STRATEGY."

"Yes, I imagine you don't usually loiter after littering a place with dead bodies."

"ANY MORE SUGGESTIONS?"

"We better call in some supplies. We've got a dozen holes to patch up and five hours to do it. In the meantime, it's time to go to the beach."

"THE BEACH?"

"Let's go find some shells."

"OH YOU MEAN GUN SHELLS."

"Quick on the uptake as usual, Asset."

Paul

"The good news is that the mouse situation is taken care of."

"You call this taken care of?"

"I just mean we don't need to call anyone or set any traps. And no dead bodies to deal with."

"Dead bodies are exactly what we're dealing with, Paul."

"In the wall. At least we don't have to see them. I know how blood makes you gag."

"Blood makes YOU gag, Paul."

"True."

"I'm gagging right now. That stench is something else."

"How many are in there? Ten? Twenty? A mass grave of mice? How does something so small smell this bad?"

"Makes you wonder about that Edgar Allen Poe story."

"Yes, Paul, that's exactly what I'm currently wondering about."

"The one about the guy who kills the other guy and hides the body under the floor. The cops come over and don't suspect anything until the killer confesses because he thinks he hears the dead dude's heart beating."

"*The Tell-Tale Heart.*"

"Yeah! That's it! Makes you wonder."

"About human psychology? About the nature of guilt?"

"No—about why the cops couldn't smell the dead guy."

"Good point."

"Sour tiny mouse corpse stench wafts right through the wall and into our nostrils—shouldn't the victim in that story have reeked?"

"Maybe the officers had head colds."

"That's not a bad idea."

"What?"

"Know anyone who's stuffed up? Maybe we could ask them to cough in our faces."

"Our daughter. Thanks to daycare, she's always stuffed up."

Agent E

"Let me get this straight, Agent E."

"Ma'am?"

"There were rodents in the wall."

"Affirmative, ma'am."

"And the Asset shot up the wall."

"Riddled it, ma'am. Turns out perforating a wall with bullets really does kill whatever's on the other side, action movies be damned."

"And you spent the rest of the night patching up the wall so your mom and dad would neither ask nor solve this riddle."

"An apt turn of phrase, ma'am."

"I still don't get it."

"Ma'am? Your rundown matches the sequence of events."

"Why the stench?"

"Decomposition, ma'am. The corpse's cologne. Death's deodorant. Post-life perfume. Decay bouquet. The sour scent of—"

"Do you think I'm asking why a dead body smells?"

"Aren't you, ma'am?"

"I'm in charge of spies and assassins. You don't think I know that a dead body smells?"

"My apologies, ma'am."

"I'm wondering why you didn't remove the corpses, Agent. Before you patched up the wall. Why not toss the critters in a dumpster and be done with them?"

"My mother wants to move, ma'am."

"Is that an answer to my question?"

"Old Boots is dragging, well, his boots."

"Ahhhhhh. Now I get it. Smell him out, is that it?"

"You've alighted on the gist of it, ma'am."

"The old stink bomb maneuver."

"Just doing my job, ma'am."

Paul

"It's official. Amy and I are never having sex again."

"I thought you were going to get back to it when the kid left for college."

"Not anymore."

"What happened, bro?"

"Manhattan happened."

"The place?"

"The dog."

"What dog?"

"Alex and Tom's."

"Alex and Tom's dog is named Manhattan?"

"Yes."

"Alex and Tom's dog is the reason you'll never have sex again?"

"Yes."

"Are you going to expound or should we just move on to sports or something?"

"We're dog sitting."

"Okay..."

"Grandma is babysitting."

"Dog in the house, but no kid in the house. Got it."

"Amy and I decided to take advantage of the situation. We figured Manhattan would be less concerned with what we were doing than our child."

"Let me guess. Manhattan started crying from the other room."

"No. Well yes, but that wasn't the problem."

"Manhattan came into the room? Jumped on the bed?"

"Yes and yes. And then he started licking my knee."

"What?"

"I slipped on the ice during my last run. Apparently dogs like the taste of open cuts. At least this one does. He went to town on that knee."

"Weird."

"It tickled. But that's not the problem either."

"It's not?"

"Nope. We persevered. The problem was the next day."

"Did you still have Manhattan?"

"We have him for the rest of the week. That next day—"

"After the licking . . . "

"We took him on a walk. At some point he got in his crouch and started straining."

"Taking care of his business."

"Except the thing that emerged wasn't brown. It was white. He strained and strained and the white thing stretched and stretched."

"Wait. You're telling me the dog was pooping out . . . "

"The condom. My condom. He must have gone through the trash and swallowed it whole. But no matter how hard he strained, he couldn't quite . . . detach himself from it. So I had to help."

"Dude."

"I had to pull my condom out of Manahattan's rectum."

"At least the kid didn't have to witness that."

"Saw the whole thing. Grandma had dropped her off that morning. We were on a nice family walk."

"What did she say?"

"She asked, 'What is that?' 'That, kiddo, is material evidence of the last time your parents will ever have sex.'"

"You didn't say that. And something tells me you'll persevere again."

"I thought it. And I'm not so sure you're right."

Paul

"Hey, man. PSA: veterinarians are a bunch of propagandists and liars."

"Good to know."

"Seriously. The evidence of their treachery is clear-cut and damning."

"Duh. Everyone knows that."

"I'm serious. As you know, we've been dog sitting for the last week."

"Manhattan."

"The dude's a spazz."

"He's a high-energy canine?"

"Whoa. That's EXACTLY how the vet put it. Are you . . . in cahoots with them? Is this a grand conspiracy? A cult?"

"Heather and I are thinking of getting a dog."

"And you're thinking of getting a spazz?"

"We're considering whether we have the capacity to give a high-energy canine the exercise it requires."

"Jesus. Is there an echo in here. That's word for word what the doc said on the phone. Is there a script you're both reading from?"

"Why were you calling the vet? Were you worried about Manhattan's health?"

"We were worried about our walls. Manhattan was literally bouncing off them. He also bounced off our daughter a few times, so I worried I was going to kill him."

"What kind of dog is Manhattan?"

"Mutt."

"What kind of mutt?"

"Big. And spazzy."

"How old?"

"Two? Five?"

"It probably needs to stretch its big legs."

"So said the doc."

"Did the doc suggest how you might accomplish this?"

"The doc suggested hunting."

"Hahaha."

"You don't need to laugh so quickly. I could hunt."

"Uh huh. Any other suggestions?"

"Taking it on runs. The good news, the doc said, is that dogs may be faster than humans, but they don't have our stamina. No animals do, he said. Humans have the best stamina in the animal kingdom. That's how we hunted back in the day. Before we had guns. We would track other, faster animals for miles and miles until they finally lifted their paws and waved a white flag."

"Stamina is the lamest super power ever."

"Especially since it's a filthy rotten lie."

"You don't have more stamina than Manhattan?"

"This is the fourth day I've taken him on a run. No, scratch that. It's the fourth day he's taken me on a run."

"How far do you run?"

"I wouldn't say I run. I gasp for air. I suck wind. I get side cramps. Then, when I get home, I keel over for hours on end. I'm talking to you right now while lying in the fetal position in our entry way."

"And Manhattan?"

"Still hasn't broken a sweat."

"How are your walls?"

"Intact. But only because Manhattan keeps bumping his nose into me instead of the walls."

"Awww. He's worried about you."

"I think he's checking my vitals. He's waiting to chow down on my expired carcass."

"You'll be fine."

"He IS a hunting dog. Maybe I'm prey."

"It just occurred to me. We really do have more stamina than dogs."

"Have you been listening? I'm about to croak."

"That's the thing. You're not. But he is."

"He is?"

"Comparatively speaking. Dogs have shorter life spans than humans."

"Good point. If I want Manhattan to settle down, I just have to wait ten years. He'll either be dead or geriatric."

"See? Veterinarians aren't liars after all."

"Brilliant. Now if you'll excuse me, I'm going to pass out for a decade."

"Might want to put a mirror under your nose so the dog can see you're still breathing."

Paul

"That yawn was epic, bro."

"Sorry. Daughter got me up like five times last night."

"What? She's still not sleeping through the night? Isn't she supposed to be sleeping through the night by now?"

"Talk to her, not me."

"Have you tried—"

"Yes."

"How about—"

"Yep."

"What about—"

"Uh-huh."

"I'm getting the sense you've tried everything."

"Trust your senses."

"And you want certain people to stop giving advice."

"All people."

"Because nothing works?"

"One thing works. Driving."

"Well there you go."

"Zonks out after a few minutes in the car."

"So why are you yawning? Cruise around for a few minutes and then crash. I mean, sleep. At home. In your bed. Crash was a bad choice of words."

"No good."

"No good?"

"Nope. The dog wakes her up the second we step back into the apartment."

"Barking?"

"The most reliable intruder alarm on the market."

"Or just excited to see you."

"Either way, the kid hasn't got a chance. You know how nuclear plants are always melting down in movies? The red flashing lights? The blaring honking? The robot voice telling everyone how long they have to evacuate?"

"Yeah."

"Calming a barking dog and a screaming kid and a just-woken-up wife is way more stressful."

"I bet. So, just let me finish, have you tried—"

"Taking the dog with us in the car?"

"Exactly. No intruder alert when you return."

"No good."

"No good?"

"Last night I managed to get the baby in the car seat and the dog sitting shotgun."

"Nice."

"The baby fell asleep."

"Okay."

"Even the dog plopped down to take a snooze."

"Mission accomplished."

"Then the alarm sounded."

"The dog started barking again?"

"No, the literal alarm. The seat belt alarm. The car sensors thought the dog was a person and had a tizzy fit about him not buckling up."

"Kid woke up?"

"Of course."

"Did you try--"

"Buckling the dog in? Of course. But it turns out dogs aren't shaped like humans. I almost swerved us off the road trying to get the seatbelt around him."

"Yeah . . ."

"What?"

"Nothing."

"WHAT."

"I know you're not looking for advice."

"Spit it out."

"I mean, you don't have to actually buckle the dog in."

"What do you mean?"

"You can just click the seatbelt into the buckle—you don't need to pull it around the dog."

"That's . . ."

"Paul? You trailed off. You okay?"

"I didn't think of that."

"You're welcome?"

"I thought I'd thought of everything."

"You're on no sleep."

"Yeah."

"Maybe now you can get some."

"Yeah."

Paul

"Annnnnnnnnnd we have a dog."

"I already knew that. You have Tom and Alex's dog."

"We have what used to be Tom and Alex's dog but is now our dog."

"They gave you their dog?"

"All that's left to do is change the address on his collar."

"What happened?"

"Alex's rash went away."

"Alex had a rash?"

"Apparently. And he tried everything—every cream—and nothing worked. Even had a few shots, which were expensive and his health insurance wouldn't cover. It's a very involved story that both he and Tom told at length."

"They never told me about Alex's rash."

"Apparently they either keep it on the down low or tell the unabridged version. There's no in-between. Feel free to call them. I'm sure they'd be happy to tell you all about it as well."

"Pass."

"Anyway, it went away."

"The rash?"

"The rash. A couple days away and the rash cleared up like that. I snapped my fingers—not sure you could hear that over the phone."

"So the dog's the culprit."

"That's what they're thinking."

"And your family came to the rescue."

"Amy insisted on it."

"You don't sound overjoyed."

"It's a dog. I like dogs. Not thrilled about all the vacuuming, though."

"It sheds a lot?"

"Big-time. And I think Amy's allergic to him?"

"She is?"

"No rash, but I see her itching."

"Is she aware she might be allergic to him?"

"I think so. She stops scratching as soon as she notices me watching. Like she wants to keep it a secret."

"So you won't get rid of the dog?"

"Exactly."

"The vacuuming. The allergies. You don't sound overjoyed, but you don't sound underjoyed either. How come?"

"I mean, our place is two and a half rooms, so it's not like the vacuuming will take that long. Besides, Manhattan reminds me how great Amy is. She puts up with his dander like she puts up with me."

"You think she's slightly allergic to you?"

"To my personality? Sure. And I don't blame her. I'm allergic to my personality sometimes too."

"Ha."

"If she can love me in spite of me, I can tolerate a family hound."

"Nice."

"No matter how many condoms he poops out."

"If he poops them out, that means you've been using them, am I right?"

Paul

"Manhattan was a set-up."

"You're talking about your dog, right?"

"I'm talking about my Trojan Horse."

"Does your Trojan Horse bark and play fetch?"

"My Trojan Horse needs a stable."

"I'm not sure I know what we're talking about, bro."

"Manhattan. The dog. The dog that isn't just a dog."

"He's not? What is he?"

"A ruse."

"Is that a kind of horse?"

"A stratagem. A trick."

"I'm still not sure I know what we're talking about."

"Yesterday Amy said, 'Manhattan is a big dog.'"

"Okay."

"Okay?"

"Is that all she said?"

"It's all she said. But it's not all she meant."

"What else did she mean?"

"She meant Manhattan is *too* big."

"Too big for what?"

"This apartment."

"Okay."

"Okay?"

"He *is* a big dog. You said so yourself. Does your apartment even allow dogs that big?"

"What do you mean? You think the landlord is prejudiced against big dogs?"

"Most apartments have a no-dog policy or at least a size maximum, I think."

"Why didn't you tell me? Why didn't Amy tell me?"

"Maybe this one doesn't have a policy like that."

"Or maybe it was all part of Amy's secret plan to make us move. First she tried having a kid. Then she tried rodents in the walls."

"You make it sound like she put the rodents there herself."

"Now *this*."

"Would that be so bad? It *is* a big dog for such a small apartment."

"Might as well be as big as a horse."

Paul

"I love my wife. We are soul mates and our bond is eternal."

"So you've forgiven her for wanting to move out of a shitty apartment?"

"Water under the bridge. Love conquers all."

"Glad you made up, bro."

"You could say that. Then again, you can't make up a love like ours. It is real and it is beyond the powers and scope of the human imagination."

"Flowers. You got her flowers. Or she got you flowers. There was an exchange of plants."

"Ew. Our love is not a Hallmark card."

"Sorry. For a second I forgot how you feel about cards. In that case . . . you had make-up sex?! She finally read one of your romance novels and you both shared what you'd learned. Is that what you're telling me?"

"Even better."

"Better?"

"My kid was taking a bath and I was trying to convince her I had the Force. I've been training her to be a Jedi—did I tell you that?"

"No, but awesome. Proceed."

"She knows what Jedi can do. She takes a deep breath, feels the force flow through her, exhales, and launches herself off couches and chairs. When she lands, I taught her to roll, grab a plastic bat and pretend it's a lightsaber, and use it to knock away whatever stuffed animal I throw at her."

"The Force is strong with this one."

"That's what I always tell her, but lately she's been doubting her abilities. She's been doubting *my* abilities. If I'm a Jedi master who can train her to be one too, then where's my light saber? I told her I'd ordered it a long time ago, but it got lost in the mail. Like her LEGO set that never arrived."

"Seems legit."

"I thought so, but she's skeptical. Today, during her bath, she said real Jedi can move stuff with their minds."

"She's not wrong."

"She pointed at the door. Asked if I could open it from across the room."

"Uh-oh."

"I said my moving stuff skills were rusty, so she had to watch really closely. I could make the knob wobble, but that was all. I closed my eyes, lifted my hand toward the door knob. My plan was to say, 'There. Did you see that? The handle flinched.'"

"It flinched?"

"Power of persuasion. If she wanted badly enough to believe, I figured she'd find a way to believe."

"Did it work?"

"Didn't have to. My force worked instead. My eyes were closed, but I heard the handle jiggle. I opened my eyes in time to see the knob spin, the door click and swing open."

"Amy?"

"She'd been walking by at just the right moment, heard our conversation, took matters into her own hands."

"Talk about coming through in the clutch."

"Clearly, our destinies are cosmically intertwined like Leia's and Luke's when he's hanging from Cloud City and she senses where he is and rescues him."

"Aren't they brother and sister?"

"It's not a perfect analogy."

"Glad you two could work together to play Jedi mind tricks on your daughter."

"She's no match for the dark side of the force."

"Wait. Are you trying to turn her into a Jedi Knight or a Sith Lord?"

"Do or do not. There is no try."

"One question."

"Yeah?"

"Be honest. For a split second, when that door handle started to move, did you think you really did have the Force?"

Agent E

"Why did you ask him to open the door with his mind?"

What were you hoping to accomplish?"

"Something akin to Uri Geller on Johnny Carson, ma'am."

"Uri Geller?"

"A so-called psychic, ma'am. A self-proclaimed magician."

"Oh! The guy who could bend spoons!"

"The guy who proclaimed he could bend spoons, ma'am."

"And he made an appearance on Johnny Carson's show—do I have that right?"

"Not fully, ma'am. He did not merely appear. He failed to disappear."

"He said he could disappear—vanish into thin air?"

"Not literally, ma'am. But he did say he could literally bend spoons."

"And he couldn't?"

"Not in front of a live studio audience, ma'am."

"No magician is actually magic, Agent."

"He was no magician, ma'am."

"What do you want me to call him—an illusionist?"

"A fraud, ma'am. A phony. A charlatan. A—"

"I get it. You don't like Uri Geller."

"I wasn't talking about Uri Geller, ma'am. I was talking about my father."

"Isn't that a little harsh?"

"It's objective, ma'am. The man is a no-good grifter."

"Because he pretended he was a Jedi Knight?"

"Because . . ."

"Agent?"

"Because . . . I didn't know he was pretending, ma'am."

"You . . . believed him?"

"Just a little, at first."

"Which is why you asked him to open the door."

"Ma'am?"

"Not to expose him but to confirm he really was one with the Force. And then—"

"The knob turned—"

"The door swung open and you thought your father really was—"

"Special, ma'am."

"When did you find out that—"

"I'd been conned? Hoodwinked? Bamboozled? Not until you played the recording of his most recent phone conversation, ma'am."

"Interesting."

"What, pray tell?

"Nothing. It's just . . . your father was right."

"About what, ma'am?"

"If someone wants to believe something badly enough, they will."

"Someone in general wasn't duped, ma'am. I was, specifically. I never pegged myself for such an easy mark."

"I didn't either, Agent. Which makes me think maybe you weren't duped after all."

"Ma'am?"

"Maybe your father really is a Jedi Knight. Maybe he used his Jedi mind tricks on you."

"It won't happen again, ma'am."

"I think it will."

"You think I'll believe in mystical, manipulatable magic?"

"No, I think you'll believe in him."

"Why on Earth would I do that?"

"Because you want to."

Paul

"What about soccer, Paul?"

"What about it?"

"Should I sign her up for it?"

"Is there a football option instead?"

"She's three, Paul."

"Not tackle football. Flag football."

"I don't see it listed here."

"Well, if it has to be tackle, their bones are made of rubber at that age. She'll bounce right back up."

"No football, Paul."

"I guess soccer it is then."

"Cool. Says they need coaches. Want me to sign you up too?"

"I don't know anything about soccer."

"What's there to know? Don't you just kick the ball?"

"I think there's more to it than that."

"She's three, Paul."

"Still. I don't know the ins and outs."

"But you do for football?"

"Yes."

"How? Because you watch games on TV?"

"And because I played football."

"Your parents signed you up for football?"

"What's so funny, Amy?"

"Aren't you kind of shrimpy for football?"

"Gee, thanks."

"I'm just saying. Maybe your parents should have signed you up for soccer."

"Because I'm shrimpy."

"Because then you could coach our daughter."

"I'll coach the next sport."

"How long did you play football, anyway?"

"Do you have to smirk when you say it?"

"Sorry."

"You're still smirking. Until I was a sophomore in high school."

"Why'd you quit?"

"It dawned on me that my physique was ill-suited for the gridiron."

"You were too shrimpy."

"That is correct."

Agent E

"Is the Asset there?"

"Technically speaking, ma'am."

"Snoozing?"

"He is indeed in an enforced slumber, ma'am."

"Oh, God. Don't tell me. Another tranquilizer dart?"

"Two, ma'am."

"You gotta quit doing that, Agent."

"I was lacking in alternatives, ma'am."

"Still. He can sue the agency."

"We figured it out at night, ma'am. And during the weekdays the place is empty. But his outburst today caught me off-guard."

"Was there something in particular that triggered him?"

"Soccer, ma'am."

"Soccer?"

"Indeed. My mother and Old Boots have signed me up for the pitch."

"The pitch?"

"The soccer field, as it were. The Asset has many fond memories of watching games from above packed stadiums."

"From above?"

"He flew the blimp, ma'am."

"I see. He's not planning on flying the blimp at your 3yo soccer game, is he?"

"It might be for the best, ma'am. I fear he won't be able to contain himself if he has field-side seats."

"Maybe he can stay in the car."

"Still. Metal and glass may be no match for his vocal chords."

"That's a risk we'll have to take. I don't want him siccing the shysters on us."

"So you said, ma'am."

"He's under contract, not under captivity."

"Understood, ma'am."

"Frankly, I'm more worried about you blowing our cover."

"Ma'am?"

"You're an elitely trained athlete, Agent."

"Indeed, ma'am."

"You could dribble circles around your competition."

"You're saying I should pace myself, ma'am."

"I'm saying don't. Don't dribble circles around your competition."

"Understood, ma'am."

Paul

"Kick it! Kick it!"

"Paul."

"Why isn't she kicking it?"

"You said you didn't want to be the coach."

"I didn't. I don't."

"Then why are you yelling instructions?"

"I'm not."

"You're not?"

"I'm yelling encouragement."

"Ah."

"Run! Ruuuunnnn!"

"Paul."

"Why isn't she running?"

"She's three."

"So are all the other kids. They're running."

"I just think maybe you could cut her some slack."

"Oh, God. You're right. Am I being one of those parents?"

"Kind of."

"One of those dads?"

"Pretty much."

"I'll tone it down."

"Great."

"I'll get a grip."

"Thanks."

"You see that she just sat down, right?"

"I do."

"In the middle of the field?"

"Yep."

"But I shouldn't tell her to stand up, right?"

"Not unless you're the coach."

"Which I'm not."

"Right."

Agent E

"You . . . sat down?"

"Too far, ma'am?"

"On the field?"

"You said to keep my athleticism under wraps, ma'am."

"I said not to blow your cover. I didn't say to cover yourself up with a blanket and go to sleep."

"There was neither blankets nor sleeping, ma'am."

"Might as well have been. That's what you call blending in?"

"They'll never suspect my athletic prowess, ma'am."

"You can say that again. How'd your dad take it? I bet he blew a gasket."

"The expression is apt, ma'am."

"Where's the Asset? Tell me you didn't riddle him with tranquilizer darts again."

"No, ma'am. He fell asleep in the car and hasn't yet awoken."

"Really?"

"Yes, ma'am. My theory is that he was as apoplectic in the car as Old Boots was on the sideline. He could see me playing from the window."

"See you not playing, you mean."

"Precisely, ma'am. A few minutes ago, I heard him muttering, 'Get off your keyster and give 'em hell!' in his sleep."

"Your performance on the field took that much out of him?"

"It appears, ma'am, that he too blew a gasket."

Paul

"Did she get back up?"

"What?"

"After she sat down on the field? Did she get back up?"

"Yeah."

"Well that's something, bro."

"I guess."

"Gotta celebrate the little victories like they're big ones, right? Can you see it? Can you hear it? The inspirational music swelling as she brings herself to her feet. It's like when FDR gets up from his wheel chair in that movie *Pearl Harbor*. He didn't really do that, did he?"

"I highly doubt it."

"But your daughter *did* get up. She got up and chased after the ball like a champ."

"No she didn't."

"She didn't get up?"

"She got up, but she didn't chase the ball."

"What did she do?"

"She started dancing."

"Really? Right there in the middle of the field. Maybe she could hear the inspirational music too."

"No, she just had to pee. She was doing the pee dance."

"The pee dance?"

"By now I can recognize it from a mile off. Her legs went crooked. She looked over her shoulder at me and Amy."

"And? Did she? Pee?"

"Not on the field. Proud to say I swooped into action. Ran onto the field. Scooped her up. Then kept running, with her parallel to the ground, facing the sky—it's a gravity thing. Trying to keep the pee inside. I made vrooming noises as we charged to a porta potty. Made it just in the nick of time."

"Wow. Top-notch dadding."

"That's what I thought. When she was done, I vroomed her back to the field so she could resume playing."

"And did she? Keep playing?"

"She kept pee dancing. I fell for it a couple times—more swooping in, more vrooming sounds—until I finally got it: She thought being a rocket ship was more fun than being a soccer player."

"Makes sense to me."

"Me too."

"May not have played soccer, but played you."

"Like a fiddle."

"I knew I could hear inspirational music."

Agent E

"What was with all the bathroom breaks? Were you just messing with your old man?"

"No, ma'am."

"You really had take that many leaks? A bladder infection, maybe?"

"No, ma'am."

"Then . . ."

"Old Boots was right, ma'am. He superbly simulates a flying dirigible."

"It was really that fun, eh?"

"Beats sitting on the soccer field, ma'am."

Paul

"I don't care if she's a great athlete, Amy."

"I know. So long as she's also a super spy, a silver medal is acceptable to you."

"I just don't want her to dread gym class."

"So even a bronze would be acceptable?"

"I don't want her to dread anything, Amy."

"We all dread stuff, don't we?"

"Yeah. But you know what I mean, right?"

"She doesn't have to be picked first, but you don't want her to be picked last."

"Exactly."

"But you'd kind of like her to be picked first, wouldn't you?"

"Who ever heard of a super spy with mediocre hand-eye coordination?"

Paul

"This is the weirdest scam ever."

"What is?"

"Like, I'm used to African princes hitting me up for my credit card, but this one is so personalized. It says it's a journal about education in America and they want to publish my article."

"Really? That's good, right?"

"That's what I mean. If I'd written an article, it would probably be about American education. And if this journal were real, it would probably be the kind of place I'd submit it to. I've never gotten such personalized spam before."

"Let me see that."

"No, Amy don't click on the link. What are you—"

"Looks pretty legit to me."

"I didn't write an article, Amy."

"They've attached the text of your article to the email. See?"

"Jesus, Amy, don't open the—"

"You didn't write this?"

"Wait—yeah, those are my words. I didn't write an article, though. That was a Facebook post."

"Looks like an article to me."

"How did they get it? Do they go trawling through Facebook looking for content to reproduce? Isn't that kind of creepy?"

"You don't sound creeped out."

"I'm . . . getting published."

"You're getting published!"

"Don't get too excited. The email doesn't mention payment."

"I'll be as excited as I want to be. You're going to be a published writer!"

"This whole thing is weird. They even have a bio for me that includes where I work and the city I live in. Maybe they got it from my LinkedIn profile or something."

"Definitely surreal."

"More like Big Brother-y."

"You continue to not sound creeped out."

"My real big brother isn't scary—maybe this one isn't either."

"What are you doing?"

"Calling said big brother. He should know there's a real author in the family."

Agent E

"Good thinking, Agent!"

"Ma'am?"

"Huzzah!"

"To what do I owe your hosannas, ma'am?"

"Don't be modest."

"I really don't—"

"Don't be coy."

"Seriously, ma'am, I—"

"You know what you did, Agent."

"Tell me anyway."

"Gave your old man a much-needed boost."

"He did need a boost, ma'am, but—"

"Sure he did. Published author! That's some fancy footwork, Agent."

"No, ma'am."

"No?"

"You didn't do some behind the scenes handiwork? Tip the scales, so to speak?"

"Negatory, ma'am."

"You're telling me someone really did comb Facebook posts and find his—then offered to publish it?"

"So it would appear, ma'am."

"Crazy."

"I don't disagree, ma'am."

"Still."

"Ma'am?"

"Wouldn't hurt to give the guy a nudge, would it?"

"A nudge?"

"Sure. Do something to scooch him toward success? Without him knowing, I mean."

"I don't fix fights on another's behalf, ma'am, especially without their knowledge. If someone's going to take a fall, I don't want my client to falsely credit their own fist."

"Oh for heaven's sake, Agent. He's not just your client. He's your father. And I'm not asking you to bribe anyone to go 'Timber!' Just find a way to remind the guy now and again that he has options."

"How do you suggest I do that, ma'am?"

"Can you hack into his computer?"

"I dusted his keyboard for his prints the moment I arrived, ma'am."

"Google 'teacher training programs' and 'law schools.'"

"Then what, ma'am?"

"That's it."

"It is?"

"Have you ever searched for something one time, then found yourself flooded with advertisements for that thing?"

"Sometimes I've merely spoken about an object before it pops up in my feed."

"Right? I can't prove it, but I swear my computer reads my thoughts."

"Who needs spies with cloaks, ma'am, when our computers can read our minds?"

"Shhhhh. Don't say it so loud. Don't even think it. You'll put us out of business."

Paul

"Hey, man. Did you hear the good news?"

"No--what's up?"

"Peyton Manning can't open a can of soup."

"Oh, no. The neck stuff?"

"What?"

"I remember he had the injury to his neck. Did he lose his fine motor skills or something?"

"No. Nothing like that. He's just incompetent!"

"Really?"

"Yep! He can't figure out what clothes to wear, either! Or how to order Chinese food!"

"Let me guess. His wife has to do these things for him?"

"And his mom. But don't ruin this for me. I'm inspired. Makes me feel as though it's okay to suck at basic things in life."

"That doesn't sound like inspiration, bro. It sounds like enabling. The enabling of male mediocrity. No offense."

"I do take offense. As a mediocre man, I take deep offense."

"You are truly mediocre."

"Thanks, man."

"So am I. I'm just saying, you're not Peyton Manning. You can't throw 60-yard spirals."

"Actually, considering he's a Hall of Fame QB, Manning didn't throw that many spirals."

"Are you saying you throw better spirals than Peyton Manning?"

"I'd have to go back and look at the tape. Like Manning, I'm obsessed with studying film."

"You mean watching YouTube sports highlights?"

"Of course."

"If you discover he did, in fact, throw the football better than you, you might want to avoid asking your wife to open a can of soup."

Paul

"We bought a house."

"Whoa. That's huge, bro."

"It totally is. The house, I mean. It's huge."

"Really?"

"I think so. Amy says any house would seem huge compared to the apartment we've been living in."

"True."

"That's the thing. It's not true. Two and a half rooms is more than most people in human history have had to live in."

"You think Amy is referring to human history?"

"No—but shouldn't she? Shouldn't all of us? What does it even mean to say we need more room when we already have more room than the human race has lived in for most of its existence?"

"So you're saying we should all continue to live in caves because that's what our ancestors lived in?"

"It's not just our ancestors. It's right now. Most people in the world—most people right here—can't afford a house. Or even rent. And we're buying a house?"

"So you don't like the house?"

"I love the house. And the backyard. And the long driveway. First order of business will be installing a basketball hoop."

"So . . . congrats?"

"Thanks, but, like, congrats for what? For keeping our jobs when lots of people are losing theirs? That's why we were able to get this house. Everyone is selling their houses right now, which drives the prices down, which makes houses cheap for the few of us who have any money."

"Is that what happened? Was this a foreclosure?"

"No."

"Are the last owners on the street?"

"No, an elderly couple. Lived here since the fifties. Raised their family here. They're moving to Arizona, I think."

"There you go."

"Still."

"Still what?"

"It's gross. There's something blood diamond-y about getting a house, you know?"

"Blood diamond-y?"

"I had a place to live. A whole lot of people don't. A lot of people need a roof over their heads. What right do I have to upgrade mine?"

"How does you not getting a house help others who don't have one?"

"It doesn't. But—"

"You think that people who can't afford a house are against you getting one?"

"No. But—"

"Them wanting a house isn't the same as them wanting you not to have one."

"You sound just like Amy."

"I get what you're saying, believe it or not. I bet Amy does too. We all need to figure out a way that everyone can have a roof over their heads. But we're not any closer to that goal because you deprive yourself of a yard or a driveway."

"Or a screened-in porch."

"You got a screened-in porch? Nice!"

"I'm just asking us to have a little perspective."

"I think that's what Amy's asking too."

Paul

"Hey, bro."

"You know the best part of moving?"

"There's a best part?"

"Accidentally dropping a box down the stairs."

"A heavy box, I hope. The light ones are usually fragile."

"Dropping a light box down the stairs, wincing because you think it's probably full of fragile things, but then, instead of hearing shattering noises, hearing BEEP!"

"Beep?"

"And BONG!"

"And bloop?"

"Definitely BLOOP."

"Kids' toys? You dropped a bunch of kids' toys?"

"All the way down the stairs, one step at a time."

"Ha."

"I kept waiting for Wile E. Coyote to fall out of the box."

"Still shaped like the box?"

"Exactly. With circles spinning over his head."

Paul

"Oh, no."

"What is it, Paul?"

"We can't get this house."

"We already did get it."

"There's gotta be some way to back out."

"What's wrong? Did the inspection miss something?"

"The tree, Amy. How did I not notice before? Just look at it—standing there taking up space."

"You're against . . . trees?"

"Not on principle. In practice."

"You don't like shade?"

"It's not that."

"Or the ability to breathe?"

"Yeah, yeah, yeah. Trees are the lungs of the world or whatever."

"So . . ."

"Mowing, Amy. Trees disrupt my mowing."

"Your mowing."

"One second you're moving in nice, straight lines, then BAM, you have to swerve around a trunk."

"Sounds awful."

"It's disruptive of my Zen state."

"Hadn't thought of your Zen state."

"When I'm mowing, I like to zone out, you know? The straight lines let me do that."

"When have you ever mowed a lawn anyway? We've been in an apartment."

"You act like I was never a teenager with a summer job, Amy. I had a life before you, you know."

"Tell you what. I'll do the mowing."

"What? That would be even more disruptive."

"Of your Zen state."

"Exactly. I'd never even get into it."

"It being your Zen state."

"Correct."

"It's a conundrum."

"Maybe we could ask the sellers to chop it down."

"Or maybe we could plant, like, 50 trees."

"I don't think that would solve the problem."

"Sure it would. Instead of straight lines, you could go in little circles all over the yard. Around and around the trunks. I bet that would allow you to Zen like you've never Zenned before."

"You're mocking my Zen."

"No. I'm mocking you."

Paul

"Oh, no."

"What now, Paul?"

"The tree."

"This again?"

"It's an apple tree, Amy."

"Really?"

"Don't smile like that, Amy."

"It's charming, isn't it?"

"No."

"Apple pies, apple crisp. Maybe we could learn to make apple sauce!"

"I don't know how to make apple sauce. Do you know how to make apple sauce?"

"I said I could learn."

"Sounds good to me. Does that mean you'll pick the apples before they fall?"

"Just had an image of taking one right off the tree. Rubbing it against my shirt sleeve. Taking a bite. Completely charming."

"Bucolic."

"You think they're diseased? You think they'll give us a disease?"

"Not bubonic. Bucolic. It means quaint, I think. From the country."

"You don't look so good yourself. Are you shivering?"

"Shuddering. I think I just heard an apple plop to the ground."

"Oh, c'mon. The plopping of apples is that traumatic?"

"Let the record show, I'm not picking them off the ground, Amy. I'll mow them before I pick them."

"Is that what this is about? Your mowing again?"

"No. Not my mowing. My Zenning."

"And apples disrupt your Zenning too?"

"They delay it."

"How long is the delay?"

"However long it takes to get on my hands and knees and pick up the apples."

"I thought you said you're not going to do that."

"I'm not."

"Can a lawnmower mow apples? Where are you going?"

"To get the lawnmower.

"Right now? You're going to mow right now?"

"I prefer to think of it as making apple sauce."

Paul

"There you are, Paul."

"I'm definitely here."

"What are you doing down there?"

"You're serious? I'm picking up apples."

"Still?"

"Still."

"I thought you were going to mow the lawn."

"I WAS going to mow the lawn. I AM going to mow the lawn."

"What happened to mowing over the apples?"

"The lawn mower objected strenuously to this idea."

"Is it okay?"

"TBD."

"TBD?"

"To be determined."

"I know what it means. Wondering when it will be determined."

"After I'm done picking up these apples."

"Sorry, Paul. Do you want some help? We can totally help when we get back."

"Get back?"

"Come with us."

"Come with you where?"

"Oh. Right. That's why I came out here. My mom invited us."

"To do what?"

"You know what? Never mind."

"Amy."

"Go to the apple orchard."

Agent E

"What is that infernal thumping?"

"Apologies, ma'am."

"Wait. It's you? You're the one making that racket?"

"Mea culpa, ma'am."

"All night long. Thump, thump, thump in my earpiece."

"I should have turned off my own earpiece, ma'am."

"What on earth are you doing, anyway?"

"Shooting."

"Shooting? Your laser gun?"

"Apples, ma'am."

"In the middle of the night? Is the Asset throwing them into the air for you?"

"Negatory. He isn't here, thank goodness. As you say, ma'am, it's the middle of the night. Nor am I shooting at apples, ma'am. I'm shooting apples. Like shooting a basketball into a hoop, ma'am."

"Why are you shooting apples into a hoop?"

"Not a hoop. A yard waste bin, ma'am."

"Same question."

"It relaxes me. Clears my head of extraneous noises."

"The Asset's a talker, isn't he?"

"Neither filtering nor modulating his voice is his forte, ma'am."

"Best—"

"Pilot in the world. Yes, ma'am. So you've told me."

"Did they have to order the yard waste bin separately?"

"I took the liberty of ordering it myself, ma'am. Old Boots is inordinately anxious about the apple situation. Thought this might ease his burden. Give him a boost, as you put it."

"Didn't they find it fishy, a waste bin just showing up?"

"They haven't yet noticed it, ma'am."

"What do you mean?"

"They can be a bit absent-minded. Old Boots in particular."

"Well, at some point they'll have to notice it, won't they?"

"Indubitably, ma'am. But I suspect they'll merely assume the company that does their trash and recycling provides free yard waste removal."

"Definitely sounds like something a company *should* do for free."

"Precisely, ma'am."

"Come to think of it, why wouldn't a yard waste bin be standard operating procedure?"

"The 's' in *yard waste* is a money sign, ma'am."

"Ha. Anyway, nice of you to help your father out."

"Merely executing my mission, ma'am."

"Professional courtesy is still courtesy, Agent."

"Very true, ma'am."

"But you know you have to dump the apples out, right?"

"Ma'am?"

"All those apples you shot into the yard waste bin—you have to put them back in the yard where you found them."

"Certainly, ma'am."

"He might be absent-minded enough to shrug off a new bin. But he's going to take notice if it's filled with apples. I've never heard of a company doing the yard waste removal for you—in the middle of the night, no less—have you?"

"Indeed not, ma'am. Overturning the bin at this very moment."

Paul

"I've found it."

"What?"

"The most pointless product known to humankind."

"What?"

"Contact paper."

"What?"

"Contact paper."

"No, I mean, what is contact paper?"

"I didn't know either. But it turns out it's a very big deal."

"To you?"

"To Amy and therefore to me."

"So what is it?"

"Lining. For cupboards and cabinets and drawers. Think wrapping paper, except sticky on one side. Or wallpaper. You measure it, cut it out, and stick it to the bottom of the drawer."

"You mean *you* do those things. This is the first I've heard of it."

"I mean Amy does those things. I'd never heard of it until today either. Now I'll never hear the end of it."

"Amy likes to talk about contact paper?"

"She likes to talk about my failure to talk about contact paper."

"She used contact paper and you didn't notice."

"Of course I didn't notice. It's designed for me not to notice. It's literally behind doors and under dishes."

"That's what you said to her?"

"I may have pointed it out, yes."

"And she said, 'Good point,' right?"

"She said I didn't have to notice the contact paper to notice she spent hours painstakingly—that was her word—painstakingly measuring and cutting it while I was wasting my time on my phone."

"To which you nodded and apologized."

"To which I pointed out that I'd read several interesting op-eds about the state of our democracy, like the good citizen I am."

"Of course you did."

"Honestly, I showed great restraint. That was better than what I wanted to say."

"Which you're going to say to me right now."

"I was wasting my time? She'd just spent hours painstakingly measuring and cutting a product that is *designed* for no one to notice. What could possibly be a bigger waste of time than that?"

"I'm glad you didn't say that."

"Well, actually, I sort of did."

"What happened to your great restraint?"

"I didn't say it right away. You know what she said back?"

"What?"

"The fact that only we would know about the paper *was* the point. It was a little thing that makes the house feel like a home. It made her feel like a homeowner, not just a houseowner."

"Makes sense."

"It does? It doesn't make any sense to me."

"Dude. I've known you since high school. We played sports together."

"So?"

"So I know about your North Carolina boxers."

"So?"

"You literally wore the same pair of boxers under your shorts during every game for good luck."

"Your point?

"You did something no one else would see in order to feel ready. Do I really need to keep explaining this?"

"Not the same thing."

"No?"

"No."

"Why not?"

"Because I wasn't the first person to wear North Carolina shorts under my game shorts. Michael Jordan did it first."

"So?"

"So he went on to become the greatest basketball player of all time."

"I can tell you think you have a point."

"They work. That's my point. There's point-blank evidence that North Carolina shorts make you better at basketball. It's called the scientific method, man."

"Ahhh, is that what it's called."

"If putting in contact paper helped Amy make more jump shots, I'd take back every bad thing I ever said about it. I'm but a humble man of science; that's what you need to realize."

"I'm getting you North Carolina contact paper for a housewarming gift."

Paul

"What's the purpose of a rug?"

"To walk on?"

"Isn't that what floors are for?"

"Didn't know you were anti rugs, bro. Didn't know anyone was anti rug."

"I'm not anti rug; I just don't think they're essential."

"Who said they were essential?"

"Amy."

"She said rugs are essential?"

"I'm paraphrasing. I want to get a basketball hoop for our driveway but she said our account was a little tight—could we do it at the end of the month instead? I was saying sure when I looked over her shoulder. At her computer screen. She was just about to finalize a purchase for a rug."

"What does the basketball hoop have to do with the rug?"

"Nothing. Except if she can order the rug, why can't I order the basketball hoop?"

"Didn't you say money was tight?"

"It's tight because she ordered that rug. Not just that one, either. Multiple. Over the last few days several rugs have arrived at our doorstep."

"Your old apartment was two and a half rooms."

"So?"

"Your new house has more than two and a half rooms, right?"

"So?"

"Just doing the math. More rooms equals more rugs."

"What's so bad about floors? Why do we need to cover them up?"

"You asked Amy that, didn't you?"

"No. Not at first. But then soon after that, yes. I asked her if we could wait until the end of the month to get the rugs so we could afford a basketball hoop now. I'm pretty sure she scoffed at me. She said rugs are communal. I said anyone could use the basketball hoop whenever they wanted. She said she wasn't postponing getting rugs so I could get my basketball hoop a few weeks earlier."

"It's only March."

"So?"

"There's still snow on the ground."

"So?"

"The floors are probably cold."

"So you're saying rugs are an essential purchase? Ever heard of socks?"

"I'm saying rugs might be more essential than a hoop."

"I can't believe we're brothers."

"Are you going to be shooting on a snowy driveway? Are you honestly saying it's essential that you have the hoop right now?"

"Yes."

"Yes?"

"What could be more essential than a hoop?"

"Maybe rugs are what she needs to make your new house feel like a home."

"That was contact paper that did that. And anyway, what if *I* need a new hoop to feel like I'm home. Hmmmm? A hoop for me is like a welcome mat."

"I think a welcome mat is like a welcome mat."

"A minitiarized rug, in other words. When did everyone get so mesmerized by the rug propaganda?"

"You don't think a welcome mat is a nice thing to have?"

"A hoop is more than nice. It's the finishing touch. No home is complete without one."

"Cool. Finishing touches happen last, right?"

"I hate you."

"Love you too, bro. Hey. Can I ask you something?"

"Is it rug-related?"

"Rugs aside, you glad you're in this house?"

"Ecstatic."

Paul

"Paul!"

"Hi, wife o' mine."

"Hi. I just—"

"Why are you breathing so hard?"

"I ran back to the house to tell you—"

"You ran? In your work clothes? I thought you were just taking our hound for a walk. Did he pull you so hard you had to run to keep up? Sorry. Sometimes I think all those runs we go on have given him the wrong idea about standard leash speed limit. It's like when you've been driving on the highway for ours, then enter a city street. Going 30 feels like going 5. Velocitization, I think it's called. Our dog's been velocitized."

"Manhattan didn't pull. I mean, he did, but that's not why I ran. Also, side note, I highly doubt you run fast enough to velocitize anything. ANYWAY. I ran because I saw the sign."

"You opened up your eyes and saw the sign?"

"Something or other and associates."

"Who sang that song again?"

"PAUL."

"Amy."

"Listen to me. The sign—it's for a law firm. Just a block from here."

"Okay."

"You probably pass it on your runs."

"Okay."

"Okay? That's all you have to say?"

"What do you want me to say?"

"The sign—maybe it's a sign!"

"The sign is a sign?"

"You know what I mean."

"No I don't."

"Maybe in a few years it'll be referring to you! Maybe you'll be one of the Associates!"

"Ha."

"Ha? No ha. Think of it. You could walk to work every day! How cool would that be!"

"I haven't even gone to law school."

"I said in a few years."

"I don't even know what kind of law they practice."

"So go ask them. They're only a block away."

"How does a lawyer get placed at a firm?"

"Another great question for them!"

"Why are you so excited?"

"The sign, Paul."

"The sign is a sign."

"Exactly."

"I think the sign might just be a sign. I have to assume the odds of working at your neighborhood firm right out of law school are astronomical."

"Dammit, Paul. Do you have a metaphorical bone in your body? The point isn't whether you end up working at your neighborhood law firm. The point is that you're living in the same neighborhood as your dreams."

"Poetic. Kind of a reach, though, don't you think?"

"YES—you will need to reach for your dreams, Paul. That's kind of how dreams work."

"I see what you did there."

"Never mind what I did. Are you going to go talk with them?"

"Sounds kind of awkward, Amy."

"Fine."

"What would I even say? What would I start with?"

"I said fine, Paul."

"It doesn't sound fine."

"It is. It's totally fine. I give up. I'm not going to put my neck out for you ever again."

"Aren't you being a little dramatic?"

"I'm done, Paul."

"Put your neck out? I mean, don't get me wrong. You're totally supportive; I get that. I do. But it's not like you've risked life and limb."

"Sure, Paul. Whatever. Have a good time not enjoying your career. I'm not lifting any more fingers. You wanna know something? I actually thought you publishing that article would light a fire under you. But I won't intervene anymore."

"Intervene? What do you mean, intervene?"

"Nothing. It doesn't matter."

"Was it you who . . . Did you . . . Did you submit my post to that journal?"

"It's fine, Paul. How many times do I have to say it?"

"You did, didn't you? You submitted the post to the journal."

"It doesn't matter. I'm retiring as your publicist. If you're going to be a lawyer or a teacher or any other job that doesn't make you miserable, you'll have to do it on your own."

"So, what? You copied and pasted my post? You hacked into my email? You passed yourself off as me? You wrote my author bio for me?"

"You'll have my resignation letter on your bedside table by tomorrow morning."

Paul

"Well, Band-Aid Bunny, looks like it's just you and me. Don't look so bummed; at least you get to ride shotgun. I'm sorry you can't stay with your partner in crime fighting, but we can't risk it. Grandma has a dog who would treat you like a chew toy. Anyway, that's all behind us now; it's in the rear view mirror. Ahead of us, the open road. Well, okay, not that open. It's 4:30 on a Friday—what did you expect? Shit. Is it that late? I was hoping to swing by that law office on my way home. Yes, really. Oh well, maybe this is better. Now I can tell Ames that I tried but traffic got in the way. How much credit do you think she'll give me just for the effort?

Probably about as much credit as the time I told her that I tried to make reservations for Valentine's Day. Look. I know. I shouldn't be going there to get credit. I shouldn't be going just to humor my wife. I should go . . . to go. To not just try but to actually do. What's the worst that can happen? They'll tell me it's not worth it—it's hard and it consumes your life and you never leave the office. Or it's dull. God, after all the nights spent studying, what if the job is just as soul-sucking as what I'm doing right now?

What if I can't pass the bar? I hate tests. I couldn't even pass my driver's test the first time. I didn't do anything wrong. Didn't hit any cones while parallel parking; didn't forget to use my turn signal; didn't break any laws. At the end of my test the guy told me I didn't pass because, before we got going, he'd asked me how I was doing and I'd admitted I was nervous. He told me a person should never get behind the wheel if they were nervous—a nervous driver, he said, was a dangerous driver. That is a TRUE story, Band-Aid Bunny. All these years later, I'm still ashamed. Not at being nervous—who wouldn't be?—but at not saying anything to the guy. Not speaking up and telling him what the hell? Not debating him and a system that would grant him that much arbitrary power. For the next three months—that's how long I had to wait to take the test again—I told people that I went the wrong way down a one-way, because that was less embarrassing than the truth: what I'd done wrong was to sit there, stunned, burning with quiet shame. And now I'm here, sitting in traffic, sitting in my car ranting to a stuffed animal, second-guessing myself and still not going anywhere."

"I HAVE A NEED."

"Wait—what did you say? Did you say something?"

"A NEED FOR SPEED."

"Band-Aid Bunny, this is crazy."

"PETAL TO THE METAL!"

"Let go of the steering wheel."

"MOVE IT OR LOSE IT, PEOPLE."

"Take it easy, bunny."

"EAT MY DUST."

"Where did you learn to drive like this?"

HONK!

"Lay off the horn."

"I HAVE A NEED."

"Yes, I heard. A need for speed. But—"

HOOOOOONNNNNKKKK!

Paul (a couple minutes later)

"Just sit back in your chair and let me do the talking, Band-Aid Bunny."

"License and registration."

"Yes, Officer."

Agent E

"The Asset will be decommissioned with haste."

"Decommissioned, ma'am?"

"If the damage can be controlled—a big if—it will be."

"Damage, ma'am?"

"My resignation letter will be submitted with equal promptness. This is my fault. I knew the risks when I assigned the Asset. His reputation preceded him. A hothead, they told me. A blabbermouth, they said. They also assured me he was the best and most versatile pilot and driver they'd ever seen. I chose talent over tact, and his tactlessness ended up being a thumb tack in the rear of this mission."

"Resignation letter, ma'am?"

"Oh, for God's sake, Agent. Quit repeating everything I say. What's the matter with you? Has your brain short circuited? You have nothing to worry about, Agent. You're in the clear. So pull yourself together, and that's an order. The last order I may ever give."

"My apologies, ma'am. I'm merely confused. Why would the Asset be decommissioned? Why would you resign?"

"You heard the tape, didn't you? Our cover is blown. The Asset commandeered your father's vehicle and didn't mince words about it."

"No, ma'am, I don't believe he did."

"The tape, Agent. It's all on tape."

"The Asset assures me he neither drove nor spoke."

"He could have fooled me."

"With all due respect, ma'am, I believe it was my father who fooled you."

"You're saying—"

"My father did the commandeering himself, ma'am. He picked up the Asset; he put the Asset's paws on the wheel; he used said paws to crank said wheel."

"But the voice . . ."

"Also my father's. A good impression of the Asset, to be sure, but no more than a facsimile."

"But how did he know how the Asset talks?"

"The ear plugs, ma'am."

"The ear plugs?"

"Now you're repeating me. Yes, the ear plugs. The ones the Asset and I have placed in my parents' ears every night. They did not just block out sound; they played it. More specifically, that played audio of the Asset talking."

"But . . . why?"

"I didn't want to have to insert those ear plugs indefinitely, ma'am. Every night for more than a year I've played audio of the Asset—first faintly, then, gradually, with greater volume. Eventually, I reasoned, the Asset would be able to, as you say, blabbermouth away and my parents would be so inured to his voice that they would remain asleep, no ear plugs required."

"So your father has been getting a steady diet of the Asset's voice in his unconscious for . . . "

"Months, ma'am."

"I'll be damned. Still."

"Still, ma'am?"

"That means your dad cracked. He thought he was a living, breathing, driving, loudmouth stuffed animal."

"To be fair, my father was always cracked, ma'am."

"Why don't you sound more upset? Your father's a wack job."

"He's always been a bit of that too, ma'am. Truth be told, I don't think this was evidence of delusion. Flight of fancy, perhaps, but not a full-blown episode. In fact, I think this may have, at long last, been a sign of true growth. He finally stopped talking about the right thing to do and did it."

"He got a ticket, is what he did."

"That too, ma'am."

"I better hang up. I have some decommissioning paperwork to, well, decommission."

"What happens when an agent gets decommissioned? Ma'am? Ma'am, you still there?"

"I better make a few calls. Make sure none of the paperwork falls through cracks."

Paul

"Paul? Where are you going?"

"When?"

"Now. When do you think?"

"Wasn't sure if you meant now or right after that."

"Let me rephrase. Where are you going at this exact moment and also right after that?"

"Now—the law firm down the road."

"You're gonna talk to them?"

"I got this hefty ticket to take care of. Thought they might be able to offer some advice."

"How about a career. Can they help with one of those too?"

"We'll find out."

"And then?"

"After I find out if I want to become a lawyer? I don't know. Lots of falling asleep in libraries, my eyes bleeding onto textbooks?"

"After you go to the law office. You said you were going somewhere else."

"Oh. Right. I have a meeting with an adviser to talk about a teaching program."

"What's gotten into you?"

"I told you, it's all Band-Aid Bunny's fault. I might bring him with me if I'm running late. He's crazy, a real loose cannon. But he might also be the greatest driver I've ever seen."

Paul and Agent E

Paul hands his 3-year-old daughter a basketball. It's a real basketball—rubber—but minitiarized. Like the ones you win at fairs if you make a shot in a too-tall, too-small rim.

They both stare at the recently-installed basketball hoop. It's not too tall or too small. It's perfect. 10-feet exactly.

Paul sighs, picks up a broom.

"Part of me," he admits (to his daughter? to himself?), "wants to keep this hoop at 10 feet. At least for the first shot. My own driveway hoop." He sighs again. "I'd like to christen it myself."

He raises the broom handle and uses it to click on a latch behind the backboard. The hoop lowers.

Chin-height for Paul, though his daughter still needs to crane her neck a bit.

"But this isn't just my hoop," Paul says. "It's ours. It's yours. That's why I got an adjustable one. And it's why I want you to have the first shot." He puts his hand out, in front of the ball his daughter is holding. "Hold up. Let's make this as dramatic as possible. A buzzer beater. I'll set the timer on my phone for ten seconds. I'll count down out loud. When I say one, you shoot, okay?"

His daughter nods without taking her eyes off the rim, her mouth curling into the faintest of smiles.

"Okay. I'm setting my phone for 10 sec. . . oh, great. Looks like someone responded to my Facebook post. Sorry. I need to read this. See what this guy . . . Oh my God, is this guy serious? He's gotta be trolling, right? He can't honestly think that's a winning reply. That's his salvo? Just hold on a second, okay, kiddo? I've got to respond to this. I can't not respond. I should. I should *not* respond. It would be way better for my health. But then again . . ."

His daughter keeps eyeing the rim. But the smile is gone.

Agent E

"Ten!"

"Is this really necessary, Agent?"

"Undoubtedly. Nine!"

"He's made progress. He has."

"I concur. Eight!"

"He's taking steps to improve his life."

"Affirmative, ma'am. Seven!"

"He's slowly but surely becoming a better husband."

"Inarguably, ma'am. Six!"

"A better father too."

"Indubitably. Five!"

"So why not put the phone down, Agent."

"No can do, ma'am. Four!"

"Sure you can. Put the phone down, close the lid, and walk out of the bathroom."

"Negatory. Three!"

"You said so yourself. He's trying. Your hard work is paying off. Your mission may be ongoing, but you should be proud of the work you've done so far."

"I'm not doing this as an agent, ma'am. Two!"

"You're not?"

"I'm doing it as his daughter. One!"

"Agent? Did you make it?"

"A perfect sploosh, ma'am."

Made in the USA
Middletown, DE
14 November 2022

14869694R00179